TIGER CLAIMED

AN ISLAND STRIPE PRIDE TALE

C.D. GORRI

COPYRIGHT

Copyright 2022 C.D. Gorri, NJ

Don't forget to sign up for my newsletter here:
https://www.cdgorri.com/newsletter

DEDICATION

To the sassy ones,
Keep testing those boundaries and exceeding expectations.
No matter what anyone else tells you, remember you are the
perfect someone for some lucky sonovagun.
Xoxo,
C.D. Gorri

TIGER CLAIMED

ISLAND STRIPE PRIDE

His Tiger wants to claim her, but she wants to reveal his secret…

The Shifter Council of New York City has announced a warning to all its citizens. Danger is lurking on the horizon, and now, more than ever, the supernatural community must work to keep their secret. With increasing reports from normals of supernatural activity in the Big Apple, their entire existence is at risk.

Trench Tora is an Enforcer for the Island Stripe Pride. When his Neta sends him to investigate a vlogger claiming to have seen a man turn into a dog, he doesn't expect to be attracted to the curvy beauty. More than that. He thinks she's his mate.

Bria Grotto is trying to make a name for herself among the millions of paranormal investigators out there by investigating claims of the supernatural in the big city. Just when she thinks she caught her big break, Bria finds herself hunted by the very creatures she means to catch on camera.

Should she trust the big, sexy stranger who comes to her rescue? Even if it means giving up her prize footage…

ISLAND STRIPE
PRIDE

The city was crowded. Okay, that was an understatement. Besides, he wasn't looking at the whole city. He was looking at the new meeting space the Council had procured from a group of Rabbit Shifters whose Warren owned a reputable real estate company.

Disguised as a *Wilderness Lodge*, a club founded by Shifters, which was a lot like the *Elks Club*, but as far as he knew one was entirely run by normals, the place was perfect for hosting meetings and events. Members only kept the humans out, and allowed not just Shifters, but other supernaturals in the area, to join them in a safe place.

Looked like everyone was feeling the pressure of

the modern world, judging by the nods and head shakes of those listening to a particularly loquacious old Wolf who had somehow taken the microphone. He was not scheduled to speak, but that didn't stop him. He just walked right up to the podium and started his fear mongering tirade.

"Greetings, my fellow representatives of the Shifter Council of New York City. Best city in the world," he said, winking like he was in some fucking Atlantic City dinner show.

Asshole.

"We are here today to discuss recent warnings our former leader, Chief Luani of the Luani Pride, had meted out during his last speech. As the group responsible for the most Supernaturals per square footage in the whole of the world, New York City is particularly responsible for establishing how we handle this threat from modern technology," lectured the McLeesh Pack's Alpha, Ernest Archibald McLeesh.

The Wolf was a fucking menace. And long-winded to boot. But what else did he expect from a tail chasing puppy? He'd much rather be lounging in the sun, or banging heads together for the Pride, but Trench Tora did as he was told. And he was told to attend this meeting.

The big Tiger Shifter crossed his arms and settled in for what was to be a boring and slightly inflammatory speech. The Wolf in the next seat glanced at him sideways before inching his chair slightly away. Smart man. Trench was already annoyed, but he kept his focus on McLeesh and all the older Wolf's posturing.

"The cold, hard facts, people, is that we are no match for modern technology. It is everywhere! Children have phones with recording devices! The brats are everywhere, and they are constantly taping everything and putting it on the web and apps for the entire world to see," he sneered.

"Christ, will this bullshit never end?" a Fox Shifter sitting behind Trench muttered.

He had to agree with the sentiment. This was the 21st century, and Shifters were still a secret. In fact, the whole supernatural world still remained in the shadows. As a big Cat, Trench liked the shadows. It was cool and quiet there.

He had no issues with humans, or *normals* as the supernatural world referred to them. Far as he was concerned, they could do what they liked so long as they left him alone. Shifter politics were a bit more complicated than normals, given the whole secrecy thing, and it was not unusual for people like

McLeesh to use scare tactics to force their own will on the masses.

Trench hated politicians, *normal or supe*. They left him feeling dirty, slimy, and unpleasant. Not something his inner Tiger tolerated in any amount. The finicky feline preferred peace and quiet. Gatherings of this magnitude were not usually part of his job. He had no taste for it, and typically, it was not in his purview.

But when his Pride's leader, the *Neta*, gave an order, a good Enforcer like Trench obeyed. But no, he had to admit that under normal circumstances, he would never attend an open meeting of the Shifter Council of New York City without incentive or command.

Sigh.

"There is no stopping the humans. They even have cameras on people's heads. How is a Shifter to make his way unseen? Cameras on heads, hidden in car dashboards, inside traffic lights, on bicycles, and who knows where else? My own Pack Guard has taken down two would be famous internet journalists this week for trying to film what they called *unnatural healing abilities* of members of my sports clubs," the old man lamented.

Here it comes, Trench thought.

The pitch.

"As you all know, *McLeesh Iron* is a place where Shifters and other supes can go to expel their energy in this cramped fuck hole of a city. And if you mention this event, you can save 5% on an annual membership, but I digress," he continued.

His old Scottish accent had grown thicker with each syllable uttered. Made understanding him damn near impossible. Even his own Pack squinted while the other representatives from local Clans, Covens, and Prides cringed in their seats.

"Yeah, yeah. We know, McLeesh. How many times have we asked you to close it to the public, McLeesh?" a crowd heckler yelled.

Undaunted, the pompous old Wolf went on with his agenda. Trench tensed. He did not care for the man's scare tactics and his dismissal of those present. But it wasn't for him to say. He had a job, and he would do it.

"My Pack immigrated, like so many of you, from abroad. We travelled here, to these shores, many years ago, seeking security, safety, and prosperity," McLeesh added, earning some more pained groans from those in attendance. "And in that time, no other Wolf Pack has been as loyal to the Shifter Council as we. We've offered our support, given good advice, provided muscle, and yet, the Council has failed to keep us safe from this, the biggest threat we've faced from the normals."

He paused then, eyeing the crowd for dramatic effect. It set Trench's teeth on edge, but he simply sat and listened. Waiting for a signal.

"Technology is not going away, my friends, it is time for a change. Therefore, I call for a vote of no confidence in this Council's current administration---"

"Aren't you just full of piss and vinegar since we didn't vote you in as interim head?" the same heckler asked.

"True, I lost the vote," McLeesh sneered. "But what have you got in my place, then, eh? Where is this house cat, this *Neta*, of the local Tiger Pride that you voted to lead our Council?" he snarled, waving his arms as if in invitation.

The room stilled as heads swiveled to and fro. Everyone was looking for the Island Stripe Pride Neta, Dean Romero. Trench growled deep in his throat, the low-pitched infrasound causing those around him to still suddenly. It was a neat trick. His wild cousins used it to paralyze their prey, and Shifters used it in much the same way.

As an Enforcer for the Pride in question, his warning was clear. After waiting a moment, he gauged the reactions of those nearest. The smart ones backed away or shut their traps. The dumb ones went right on barking smart aleck comments, unaware that they were being hunted. That was the problem with city Shifters. Too much time spent in their human shapes, they forgot how to recognize danger.

Trench knew what they were thinking, could feel their derisive dismissal of his Pride. But he did not give a fuck. He was not there to speak, merely to listen and take note. He would only act when his Neta directed. It was what he was good at.

He heard the whispers around him and ignored them. Some knew his reputation, others only his name. Hardly anyone knew his face. Typically, because it was the last thing they'd have seen before, he would've ended them.

Trench was officially an Enforcer. But he'd earned his stripes, not the ones he was born with, by being a killer. At one time, he was one of the highest sought after assassins and best kept secret of the Shifter world for over a decade. His black ops missions were so confidential only those with the highest clearance were aware of his involvement.

"I see this kitten has not shown his face. He doesn't care about our troubles. When has a cat ever helped a Wolf?" sneered the insolent McLeesh.

Trench was getting pretty tired of this guy's tirade. Perhaps he should ask the Neta if he wanted him handled?

Grrr.

"And to answer someone's other question, earlier," McLeesh said, turning on his heel. "As you all know, we have closed our doors to the public. *McLeesh Iron* is currently *members only*. You must prove to be one of us to get your membership. These clowns, parading as journalists and reporters, looking for a quick shock and awe story to earn them a Pulitzer, will stop at nothing. The fact is, we are not safe," he said, letting that sink in.

Trench had to admit the old Wolf was wily. Some Shifters in the audience were nodding their heads, agreeing with the pompous ass.

"Now, I've called Draco Fortis, and I've asked their top programmers what they can do for us. The answer is forthcoming, but it shall take time. I believe we have been successful in keeping ourselves hidden, but we need real leadership to remain that way," McLeesh ended, arms wide.

A chaotic chorus of snarls and roars of both approval and disagreement rose from the crowd. Trench did not react, even though he was more than a mite aggravated.

An irate Scottish Wolf was a barely intelligible and volatile creature. McLeesh was egging on the crowd, and those of the Shifter Council of New York City did not need another scene. Not now.

But would that stop tempers from flaring? Apparently not. While the Wolves bickered, the Tiger Enforcer waited. His Neta had kept himself hidden on purpose. Any minute now, these assholes were going to be singing a new tune.

"It is true, technology moves fast these days," one of the Vampire representatives spoke. His name was Blake Nero, and he stood, addressing the gathering at large.

"We Vampires have been monitoring the internet for any activity, and McLeesh is right. I am loath to announce this so publicly, but we have heard something while scanning. Something of a problem concerning the Wolves-"

"See! You see. Here is the heart of our problem. We have no interspecies communication, and now Vampires are holding onto information that could out the Wolves! This is not just our fight. It is for the safety of all of us that we must act," McLeesh growled.

"Are you saying we did not tell you soon enough, dog," Blake growled.

Trench waited, then he moved quickly to the stage where the Wolf and Vampire were now snarling and shouting at one another. As soon as he reached the bottom of the stairs leading to the podium, someone stood up. The stranger tossed the dark cloak he was wearing to mask himself from the crowd off his massive shoulders, and Trench's nostrils flared, his eyes zeroing in on the man. He paused, recognition dawning, and averted his gaze out of respect and submission.

Dean Romero was the most powerful Tiger Shifter in all of New York. He was also a mate, a father, and one all around badass motherfucker. He'd been voted in as the interim head of the Shifter Council while the Lions, who made up the 135th precinct, a supernatural police headquarters operating within New York City, took care of some business.

Yes, he'd been willing to do the job, but like most things, politics were politics, and it would be easier weeding out his enemies if he laid low at first. It certainly didn't take very long. First Wolves, then Vamps. Hell, the Tiger King had a lot of work ahead of him.

That was where Trench came in. As an Enforcer, he was more than a bodyguard. He was the designated protector of the entire Pride. An investigator. A fucking warrior. He would give his life for his Neta, as he would for any member of the Island Stripe Pride. Pride was family, and Trench valued that above all else.

"You all know me," Dean Romero said without any bullshit posturing.

He took the microphone and moved between the stunned Wolf and Vampire. It was an insult, Trench knew, but he wondered if these city supes were aware. For the Tiger to so easily dismiss both representatives, it meant he didn't see them as a threat. He did not fear them. And when you were a predator, that was pretty fucking telling.

"I have been here since you began talking, McLeesh, waiting for this shit show to finish before I addressed the Council's representatives and the rest of you in attendance," Dean said, his face unsmiling.

"First, I am only the interim head of the Shifter Council of New York, and I am only that because I was asked. For all of you who think I am out to keep this job permanently, please hear me when I tell you this is not my idea of a good time," he paused, allowing those who laughed or applauded to quiet down.

"My mate and I are quite content running our Pride, and I am not looking to make this position permanent. A proper vote for the new Chief Head Officer of the Shifter Council of New York City will take place at the usual time next year," Dean Romero said in a clear voice that belied his true Alpha nature.

He was trying for friendly, but the Tiger Shifter simply radiated power. Six and a half feet of iron muscle and eyes that glowed with his beast gazed at the gathered audience. The Island Stripe Pride's Neta was all leader, a true Alpha male, and Trench Tora was proud to be his Enforcer.

He owed everything to the Pride and would do whatever was requested of him without fail. He owed Dean that much. Trench turned and growled at some of the folks around him who'd started whispering, and they quieted immediately.

Smart fellas.

He would broker no disrespect aimed at his Neta. His inner Tiger would not allow it. Predatory Shifters such as they were hard-wired to demand submission and obedience from their lessors. And when it came to Tigers, just about everyone was lesser.

Grrr.

"I am stepping in for Captain Luani until things at the 135th precinct get sorted. That means, if you have a problem, you come to me. With the city's rampant budget cutting among law enforcement, the captain has to go where he is most needed. I think we can all agree, that is where he can best serve the supernatural community of New York. I swore an oath to this Council and to all of you I shall work to the best of my ability to keep things running smoothly until the official vote," Dean said, addressing all concerns and questions evenly and to the best of his ability.

As far as Trench was concerned, that was good enough for him. His Neta's word was law, and he had no doubts the man would do his best for all of them. Dean Romero was a fucking god among Tigers, and Trench was proud to be an Enforcer for the guy.

"Now, we have a Wolf problem, let's fix it. Blake, McLeesh, I will send my best to investigate the circumstances you presented. We will have an answer as soon as possible."

Then Dean's gaze landed on Trench, and he knew

what was being asked. Without hesitation, Trench nodded. He would get the details from the Vampire and start immediately. After all, that's what an Enforcer does.

Grrr.

CHAPTER ONE

ISLAND STRIPE PRIDE

"Bria! Did you change the laundry yet?"

"Oops! I'm on it," she replied, closing her eyes in annoyance.

Shit.

Bria had been living in the three-bedroom apartment in the affordable, but barely secure Madison Arms for about nine months now. And yet, she still wasn't used to Nancy. The woman was one of her four roommates', and she was sort of infamous for lurking.

Truly, Nancy was like the villain in a B horror movie with the way she popped up in the weirdest places. And completely out of nowhere, too. Even worse was her rigorous chore schedule she insisted on meting out to the entire group of them.

Always on a deadline, Bria had to admit, she was slacking when it came to organization. But she'd set an alarm this time. Maybe Nancy was wrong. Sighing, she looked up from the article she was typing.

Damn it.

She really was late getting to the laundry room. The neon numbers on the microwave clock didn't lie. She should have switched machines ten minutes ago, and that was bad. It could mean the difference between heaven and hell for their poor bath towels.

Lurking in the depths of the hallways was the villainous, the heinous, the always nosy Mrs. Garcia. She lived on the second floor but roamed all of them daily in her quest to write the most complaints a single person could have, to the company who owned the building. She complained about everything. Litter on the floors, inappropriate door decorations, and worst offense of all, clothes left in either the washer or dryer.

Mrs. Garcia was like the Madison Arms Apartment Complex's own laundry room police. The woman was a freaking nuisance. No one liked her. Well, except for Nancy. The tiny blonde was tapping her shoe and glaring at her smart watch as Bria clicked save on her document. She stood up, noticing with a perverse amount of pleasure the way

Nancy winced as the chair scraped on the linoleum floor.

"Well?" the blonde asked.

"I'm on it, Nancy," Bria replied, smile and all.

Dashing across the room, Bria grabbed her cell phone and keys before running out of the apartment towards the elevators. The laundry room was located in the basement of the older building. They were fighting to keep their costs under the same rent control laws that had been established back when the original owners erected the place close to seventy years ago.

Of course, in New York City, nothing was as it seemed. And the new landlords were pushing for increases that neither she nor her roommates could afford. One of them was based on the grounds that they couldn't possibly keep the place secure without renovations to security systems, new doors, and windows that were somewhere in the high hundreds of thousands of dollars.

"I already took out your towels, Ms. Grotto. Tsk, ten minutes ago. You know you are not the only one who needs to use the washers today," Mrs. Garcia snapped.

"I'm sorry, Mrs. Garcia," Bria said with a tense smile plastered to her face.

She was raised to be polite to her elders, but the smile dropped as soon as the older woman shook her head and walked away. Of course, Mrs. Garcia didn't put the towels in the dryer or even in the cart.

Nope.

She'd dumped the entire load right on the grimy floor, meaning Bria would have to wash the bottom two at least one more time. And now, she'd have to wait to do that.

Ugh.

Sighing, she loaded the dryer and left the two soiled towels on top of the machine with a note to Mrs. Garcia that she would rewash them. But, just to make sure she didn't miss the next cycle, Bria decided to work from the laundry room.

Ugh.

How could anyone be so rude? She lamented the loss of her comfy seat cushion and opened the old metal folding chair that rested against the wall. A few minutes later, Jess, another one of her roommates, came bounding in with Bria's laptop, its charger, and a mug of hot coffee.

"Oh my God, Jess, I swear I am gonna name my firstborn after you," Bria sighed and took a sip of the good stuff.

Jess was a new addition to the place, but she was sweet and nice. And she didn't take any shit, which made her like Bria's idol. Even better, the woman had just gotten a promotion and was already leaving their little place for one of her own. Quite the feat in this city.

"Your firstborn? Bria, you need to get you a man first," Jess replied, shaking her head.

Bria shook hers back and gulped. Trying to date the opposite sex was a study of disappointment in her tried and true experience. She'd have better luck finding proof that the supernatural existed, which was the entire basis of her vlog.

Her website, *Lost and Found: Proof of the Supernatural in the City*, was ranked pretty high especially for such a niche audience. Her fan base was mostly American, and though she was small time, she still managed to eke out a living.

Checking the analytics tab, Bria grinned when she saw she had six hundred and fifty thousand likes on her latest video. That would score her even more paid ads. If this kept up, maybe she could leave her roommate worries behind.

"Gotta go, roomie," Jess said. "And don't let Nancy give you shit for taking long with the towels. That heifer waited all day to take her smelly ass garbage out after she made all that fish for her lunches this week too."

"I won't. Did I mention how much I am going to miss you?"

"Yep. But I am still going."

"Fine. Have a good day," Bria replied.

"Mmm hmm."

Jess shook her head and walked to the elevator, presumably to head to work. She was with the child protection services, and Bria admired her every day. It took a woman of certain strength, compassion, and grit to do that job.

The video in question had been sent in by an anonymous source and, from what Bria could tell, seemed pretty damn real.

"No way, Jess. My last date was with a guy with a Frankenstein fetish who lived in his mom's basement. Worst. Date. Ever. Anyway, I ditched him before I ended up spare parts in his freezer," she replied with an exaggerated shiver.

"You do have lousy taste," Jess concurred.

"Thanks, temporary roomie," Bria replied, waving the brat away.

After an hour and a half of washing, waiting, drying, and finally, folding the first load of bath towels, Bria had only the two that she had to rewash left in the dryer. She was clicking on her email when she noticed an anonymous tipster had sent her a video file.

Dang it.

She hated it when they did that, since video clips were sometimes computer viruses in disguise. After running it through her security software, she deemed it safe to open.

"Let's see," she murmured and opened the file.

Her heart raced, eyes wide, Bria was shocked and awed by what she saw. A man- *seemingly normal, though very tall, and very muscular in a gangly sort of way,* was stepping outside of *The Stripe Club.*

A quick search told her the place was a high end strip bar, what used to be called a *gentlemen's club.* It was located somewhere on the lower east side. Some actors, a few rock stars, and the occasional gangster were said to frequent the place.

But none of that was particularly interesting. Still, Bria continued to watch the video as it showed the stranger heading towards the alley. The amateur director was sure to take a shot of the full moon, and Bria frowned. That was weird. Then things got weirder.

The man fell. He was clutching his stomach as if he were in pain. Background traffic was loud, so she couldn't be sure, but she thought she heard a scream. Then, the impossible happened.

Holy fucking shit.

Excitement raced through her veins, and she unknowingly missed her floor. Forgetting the laundry cart in the elevator, as she stepped out into the hallway. Her eyes were riveted to the footage. She wished it wasn't so damn grainy, but she could not look away.

Bria squinted, frowning at the bad image. She clicked away at the keyboard, running the video through some software that had enhancement filters.

Then she watched it again.

And again.

And AGAIN.

"Ohmyfuckinggawd," she squeaked. "He's a Werewolf!"

A door slammed open, and she looked up.

What the fuck?

How did she end up back in the basement? And who the heck were those guys? A couple of strange men wearing all black had stepped through the door that opened up to the Madison Arms' back entrance. They were tall, muscular, and a little hairy. Kind of like the dude in the video.

Gulp.

"Who's a Werewolf?" one of the strange men asked.

"Um, no one?" she squeaked.

"Nah, this lady is too smart to believe in that nonsense. Ain't ya?" another asked.

"So, what say you hand over the laptop and come with us, eh?" from a third.

"Um, actually, my mother told me to never leave my apartment building with three large strangers," Bria said, closing her laptop and hugging it tight to her body.

"Really? Seems oddly specific from your average mom," the tallest of the trio, stepped forward.

Shivers raced up and down Bria's spine, and the hair on the back of her neck stood up. Those were exactly the warning signs she talked about on her vlog. Those tiny glimpses of a sixth sense that so many people felt when facing something unexplainable.

"Fuck, this is not good," she whispered, backing up into the wall.

"You have no idea. Now, hand it over," one of the men growled.

Like actually growled. Like a dog, *or gulp*, a Wolf.

"Um, listen---"

Just then, Mrs. Garcia, her *oh so nosy - thank fuck*

for that - neighbor, came out of the elevator. The older woman zeroed in on Bria, and of course, jumped to the wrong conclusion, bless her ornery little heart.

"Ms. Grotto, this hallway is not approved for public parties, you know. I'm going to write to the landlord about this---"

"You are so right, Mrs. Garcia, thank you so much. I'll just be going now," Bria said, grabbing the older woman's hand in a viselike grip. "You should come with me. We can go see him now!"

"What is this? What are you doing? Are these boys bothering you? Oh no, not on my watch! See here, you hooligans, you get the hell out of here or I'll pepper spray you all," the older woman announced.

"You little---"

But before the man could finish his threat, Mrs. Garcia had grabbed a can of the stuff from one of the large pockets of her well worn cardigan that for some reason smelled like mothballs, cat fur, and pepper-mints, and she let him have it right smack in his face. The man dropped to his knees, screaming, and clawing at his eyes, while his friends lunged for the two females. Bria sneezed, damn cat allergies, but she managed to pull the old woman back into the elevator before the doors closed.

The men screamed and yelled, punching and kicking at the closed doors, but it was no good. The Madison Arms had an old as fuck elevator system, and nothing was going to get those doors open.

"What is it? I could've handled them. Say, are you okay? You look pale. Gotta toughen up if you wanna live in the Big Apple, Bria Grotto."

Mrs. Garcia shrugged nonchalantly, dropping her mace back into her pocket. The action caused some of the cat fur on her sweater to stir, and Bria sneezed again.

"Thanks, Mrs. Garcia. Um, I think it's best if we get you back to your apartment. Then I think we should call the police."

What the hell had just happened?

CHAPTER TWO

ISLAND STRIPE PRIDE

T rench entered the 135th Precinct as he had a hundred times or more and headed straight for Rami Llewelyn's desk. The detective had texted him a half hour ago with a tip on some urgent information.

"Yo," Rami called, motioning for the Tiger to come to his new office.

"Moving up in the world?" Trench asked, taking note of the boxes and eco-friendly cups full of stale coffee.

"Yeah, yeah. *Cornetti?*" he offered, holding up a box of fresh pastries.

Trench eyed the delicious little delicacies made by the detective's new mate, Noemi. The woman was a terrific pastry chef and owned the most fantastic little shop called *D'Angelo's Bakery*. Trench was a regular. As a Tiger with a sweet tooth, he knew where to find all the goods.

"Thanks, man. So, you got news?" he asked, seating himself in one of the Shifter sized chairs available to him.

"Yeah. A 911 call came in a few hours ago, a young woman claiming she was attacked by three guys in her building's basement," he explained.

"That's terrible and all, but so what?"

"The so what part is my guys were tracing the lead you sent about that video evidence of the Wolf shifting behind *The Stripe Club*, and it leads right to this woman's email account. Her name is, *uh*," Rami glanced at the file on his desk. "Grotto. Bria Grotto."

"So, we think she has something to do with this video?"

"I don't know, but you know we're swamped here, and the SCNYC is supposed to be in on this," Rami said, using the acronym for the Shifter Council of NYC.

"A couple of normals went and interviewed her already, but since the attackers were gone, and she didn't mention the video, there was nothing they could do about it."

"What else do we know?"

"We know Ms. Grotto has a pretty popular vlog where she records paranormal sightings and encounters. She actually invites guests on her video blog where she conducts interviews and holds panels about what she calls *supernatural stumbles*. It's like where normals *happen upon* the likes of us. She's bright and funny," Rami remarked, grinning like the ridiculously hairy house cat most Lions were.

"Cute too."

Rami flashed him a screenshot of the female, and Trench's inner beastie seemed to still. First time that had happened to him like that and he didn't like it. Not one bit.

The woman was young, maybe thirty, and rounder than most normals. She had a dimple on the right side of her full lips. In the picture, said lips were turned up in a warm smile that reached her sparkling brown eyes. She seemed to be enjoying herself, in spite of, *or maybe because of,* the ridiculous headband with cat ears she wore on her head, along with some plastic whiskers attached to her nose.

"Cute, right?"

"Oh, yeah?" Trench asked, suddenly annoyed.

"Does Noemi think so?"

"Hey, no call to be nasty. So, you gonna investigate or what?"

Trench mulled it over for a few minutes. Tiger Shifters liked to consider things from all angles before they attacked. It was why they were such good hunters. Thorough and precise, they stalked their prey before taking them down.

Tigers didn't rely on their females like the Lions did. Nor did they allow their passions to rule them, like the Wolves. They were lethal, steady apex predators who enjoyed working alone. Trench would hunt this Bria Grotto, and he would retrieve the damning footage and ensure his kind were protected. That was his job.

"Alright, give me what you got," Trench said, taking the file and an apricot cornetto for the road.

"That's the last apricot!" the Lion growled.

Trench just grinned, popping it into his mouth, and finishing the delicious morsel in one bite. He winked at Rami and strutted out of the precinct with his file in hand.

Bria Grotto lived at the Madison Arms with a slew of roommates. She'd been vlogging for the past year or more, having only moved to NYC nine months ago from her hometown of Paramus, New Jersey. From her picture, he noted she was a curvy little human. Cute too.

What the fuck?

Trench shook his head. He must be delirious. Reading the file, he noted her interests were strongly fixed on proving the supernatural existed. And wasn't that his kind's biggest fear?

Foolish woman was in a heap of trouble. The McLeesh Wolf Pack would be out for blood, and Dean might not be able to stop them from getting it. Though the Tiger King was typically levelheaded, there were some things even he could not stop.

Shifters needed their secrets kept. After all, who wanted to live their lives in a lab? And that's what would happen. Worldwide incarceration and forced medical tests on all of his kind. No fucking way.

Was it the Shifters' fault humans forgot their origins? That they could no longer connect to the magic that had created them. Call it God, gods, some fucking explosion or what have you, it all amounted to the same thing. Creation came from the beautiful chaos that was magic.

But it wasn't Trench's job to educate the masses. It was his job to protect the Pride, and while his Neta was head of the Council, that extended to all supes. If that meant grabbing this little girl before she let the cat out of the bag, he would. Too bad though. She really was cute.

Grrr.

"Looks like you picked the wrong topic for your vlog," Trench murmured as his eyes went to the grainy image taken from the security feed of her building's back door.

The three hulking men who'd attacked her were familiar to him. Another second, and he knew why. They were Wolf Shifters. And at least two of them had been at the Council meeting.

Fuck. This was not good. This was going to get messy. He had a feeling about those kinds of things.

Dammit. Trench hated it when shit got complicated. He took out his cell phone and texted his Neta, bringing him up to speed on the turn of events.

The video has been traced to a human female, a video blogger. Some dogs are on her trail.

The phone chimed, and Trench read his Neta's reply and grunted.

Get there first. Secure the normal and get her to safety. And keep the bodies to a minimum, would you please?

Trench grunted at the last. He was not making any promises. He frowned as he reread the message. Why should his Neta care if the woman was safe? Maybe the man had grown a soft spot for humans. After all, he'd mated one.

Whatever.

It wasn't Trench's business. He was an Enforcer and would do as he was told. It was in his training. His Neta wanted him to get the girl, so he would get the girl. Period. Even if his stomach was doing cartwheels and his Tiger was chuffing for no real reason. Trench felt the hair on his neck stand up like something was about to happen.

Whatever it was, he'd be ready.

Grrr.

CHAPTER THREE

ISLAND STRIPE PRIDE

Bria threw a change of clothes in her backpack along with her travel toothbrush, laptop, chargers, and the keys to her parents' house. She was going to lie low for a few days. Hoped that things would die down, then she could work on her next vlog.

This was so big. Bigger than big. It was huge. She finally had proof that the supernatural existed. And once she shared it with the whole damn world, Bria Grotto was going to be a household name.

Eeek!

That was vaguely terrifying once she'd thought of it. Who wanted that kind of life? That was, if she survived this and lived long enough to actually become a household name.

Gulp.

Bria knew evil when she saw it. Hell, she'd lived with her mother's evil cat, Beelzebub, growing up. That thing had been a hell beast, for sure. It tore up every article of clothing she'd had in high school. Including her prom dress just hours before the event. Yeah, evil was real and lurking around any given corner.

Those guys who'd come after her were evil. Like tear your fucking face off evil. So, no, she was not about to stick around and wait for that to happen, *thank you very much.*

Her roommates were all gone, except for Nancy. But the thin blonde never seemed to date or go out on weekends. Out of all the five females sharing the three-bedroom apartment, she was not really close to any single one of them. Might be because of her ridiculous drill sergeant like division of chores and her long lists of rules.

Jess, Betty, and Crystal were all gems. Even with Jess leaving, the other two pretty much stayed out of the way. They worked all the time and only slept and ate at the apartment.

Bria liked to think they got on like gangbusters, *whatever that means.* But still, there wasn't a single one of them she would confide to about the events of the last couple of hours. And she couldn't call her mom and dad. That conversation was a one-way ticket to *crazypantsville,* which was the unofficial name for the mental health rest home where her Uncle Bruno was currently residing.

"Am I being ridiculous?" she asked no one in particular.

But no. She wasn't. Three men had attacked her, *or* tried to, but thanks to the uncanny timing of her *not so friendly neighborhood laundry woman,* Mrs. Garcia, she'd gotten away. Bria hated to think about what would've happened if she hadn't come barging in to check the machines.

More importantly, Bria was now in possession of some serious evidence that the supernatural did exist. She'd spent years trying to capture proof, first-hand, *or even second,* that there were things out there that regular people simply had no idea about.

Like Werewolves.

Gulp.

Only, Bria had never considered what would happen after she got the proof she'd been searching for. Now that she had the video, what was she going to do with it? A question that kept her pondering during the trip to the first floor in the elevator. Nancy had barely acknowledged her exit and the hasty explanation that she was visiting her folks quite suddenly.

But they weren't exactly friends, so she didn't really mind the woman. Besides, she had bigger fish to fry. Like how to stay safe while she filmed her next vlog, where she would showcase the footage and prove, once and for all, that there was evidence of the paranormal.

She needed to be careful though, else those goons might track her down. The idea that a supernatural creature would be part of something bigger had never occurred to her. Stupid oversight? Yes. Definitely.

Running wasn't her first choice, but this was the only way to stay safe. No one knew who she was or where her folks lived. She would be secure back in her childhood home. Right?

The men who'd come looking for her had been huge and wiry like the guy in the video. Their voices were deep and growly, not entirely human. More than once, she'd noted an otherworldly glow to their eyes. Yep, definitely not human. And definitely organized.

Like a group, *or* a Pack maybe since they were Wolves? Oh fuck. That was crazy. But likely. So why did she feel excited and not just scared for her life?

"Because you're an idiot, Bria," she whispered, stepping out of the apartment complex.

"I wouldn't say that."

The stranger's voice pierced the darkness, reaching her ears. He, she knew immediately it was a man, there was just no mistaking that deep rumble, sounded mildly amused. Like she was being funny or something.

Bria stopped looking for a taxi. She'd been hoping to go to the train station where divine intervention would tell her where to go. Bria was a big believer in destiny. Especially if it meant saving her ass.

This guy threw a monkey wrench into the whole works. But once he stepped out of the shadows, she couldn't say she minded. It was not every day a cover model with the body of a professional rugby player, *much better bodies than football players, in her opinion,* stepped into her life. Anyway, back to the drooling.

Hubba hubba.

The stranger exuded animal magnetism and power, and she stilled. Curiosity reigned supreme for a single moment before she remembered to be scared. She always did have less caution and more curiosity than was healthy for a too curvy girl, or so her father always said.

Anyway, this guy was frighteningly large. Easily

twice the width of the men who'd come before. She could not say why, but there was something different about him. The others had been angry and overly sure of themselves, but he seemed smarter, and cockier, too. He approached with patience and caution.

Not because he was scared of her, and she was the first to admit he had no reason to be. She could not fight and had no weapons on her person. But that wasn't why he moved like that, so calculating and yet determined not to make her startle.

He was smart, she realized. And he moved sort of like Mrs. Garcia's cat when he had something interesting in his sights. Quietly, and with all the stealth and self-assuredness of a predator. The man used precise, calculated movements. Nothing wasted in his long-legged pursuit of her.

By the time her perusal of him brought her to his eyes, Bria knew she was in trouble. The man's face was hard. Not ugly. Quite the contrary, actually. But he didn't smile and a thin scar on his chin made him look even more unwelcoming.

His lips were a straight line across his face. He had a broad forehead, high cheekbones, and a long Roman nose that alone looked like it was chiseled from marble by the hands of some master. His eyes glittered at her like two orange and gold flames burning in the darkening night.

Just like the sparklers her dad used to light on many a hot fourth of July celebration when she was a kid. Bria had always loved those things. She'd held on to them so long. And longer still. Up until they'd burned out and her tiny palms were red from the heat. She never knew when it was time to let go.

That's what her mother always said as she'd applied aloe and lidocaine spray every night on July the fourth so little Bria could finally go to sleep. Her parents used to chide her, but it was always worth the pain in the end. At least, to Bria, it was.

Holding on till the flames expired meant she got to keep them for as long as possible. Staring into his eyes, she wondered how much hurt was in store for her. But still, she couldn't look away.

"You're Bria Grotto," the man said.

It was a statement, not a question. She didn't bother to lie. He would know it. Somehow, Bria just knew he would be able to sense it if she tried to mislead him. So, she just nodded her head. Not quite trusting herself to speak.

Everything about him said danger from the width of his shoulders to the glint in his eye, and his unsmiling face. Dangerous, yes, but also thrilling. He was excitement and mystery, and something more.

"You need to come with me," he started, but something had him turning his head sharply to the right.

Bria whimpered, stepping instinctively closer to him as another made himself known. The temperature was chilly, but in her anxiety, she began to sweat.

"Well, well," another male joined them.

"You," she whispered, eyes wide.

"You know him?"

"He came after me earlier," she told the man with the bright eyes.

Bria immediately recognized the newcomer as one of the guys who'd come after her earlier in the basement of her apartment complex. She stepped even closer to the other male, trusting the guy for some reason, which was again bat shit crazy on her part.

"No need to worry yourself, *puddy tat*. We got this. Now, hand her over," the would be kidnapper snarled.

"I don't think so," *her* stranger said.

Okay, that was ridiculous, but somehow and for

some unknown reason, she had just claimed the big man as hers. Looking between them, she knew she'd made the right decision. Even though she'd only known him for about ten seconds. Yep. It was settled. Bria had designated *him of the burning eyes* as her own personal hero, and she was totally fine with that.

"Oh shit, there's more," Bria whispered.

"Don't worry. Stay close," her stranger said to her, before turning to them. "The SCNYC is taking care of this, gentlemen. I suggest you return to your little doghouse."

He replied in that same gravelly voice. Elsewhere, she'd have called sexy, but in this instance, she'd settle for authoritative. Heck yeah, something about him simply exuded power.

"Who says we need the Council involved? I bet we can take out this little tabby," another said.

The slurs were a bit beyond her, but Bria knew pissy when she heard it. She lived with four other women. There was no time to really consider all the strange back-and-forth insults. Especially since one of the men was lunging at her.

"I got you!"

"Eeek!"

She closed her eyes, waiting for the inevitable

hurt that was about to hit her. But her stranger was hella faster than that goon.

Thank fuck for that.

The monster who'd tried to grab her had claws where his hands should have been, and she hated to think what would have happened had he succeeded in taking hold of her very human skin.

Fuck. Oh fuck. OH FUCK.

Not human. Nope. But she needn't have worried. Her new personal hero spun, catching the goon by the throat in an inhuman display of strength that made her shake in her boots. He turned to face the other two men, squeezing their buddy until he was slapping at the man's branch-sized forearm.

"I said, back the fuck off," her stranger snarled back.

There was something about his growl that made even the largest of the three attackers go still. As if the warning note had somehow paralyzed them.

Scary? Fuck yes. But Bria was learning to appreciate that about him. Very much so. Especially since he at that moment took her arm and shoved her inside the vehicle that had been parked in front of her building the whole time.

The big, sexy, scary stranger got in the driver's seat a fraction of a second before the trance wore off.

But he was already gunning the engine when the trio attacked the vehicle. Bria saw flashes of fangs and claws on the men from the lights of the car. She heard them grab onto the vehicle, and the sounds of metal being torn and ripped open.

"Hold on," the man grunted, shifting into reverse.

Thud.

Scream.

Thud thud.

Silence.

Shifting the *once pretty sweet and now sadly damaged* Corvette into drive, her stranger sped off with Bria in the passenger seat.

Shit.

She was in the car with a total stranger who'd just run over three people. Well, sort of people, who were intent on hurting her. So, actually, he'd just saved her. That was okay then. Right? Sometimes, Bria logic was difficult for even her to follow.

Maybe if they introduced themselves, it would all be okay?

She thought about that for a second, watching him maneuver through the grueling traffic of New York City like someone who had frequently driven through the city. His face betrayed no emotion, and he looked no worse for wear despite the altercation. In fact, he was not even breathing heavily.

"Um, you know who I am already. So, what's your name?" she asked after a minute.

"Trench Tora."

The big man replied without taking his eyes off the road. He was singularly focused, and she supposed she should be grateful. But for some reason, she wasn't.

Hmmm. Could be the kidnapping thing, though, right?

"Where are you taking me?"

"Somewhere safe, Bria Grotto. You have my word."

"Um, nah. I'll be okay, maybe you can just drop me off here."

He did look at her then, and from his expression, she saw the answer to her request was a resounding no.

Well, poop.

"Um, you seem to know the basics of what is going on with me already," she began."

"You're Bria Grotto from Paramus, New Jersey. You have one sibling and both parents, all alive and living in the Garden State. You came to New York City about nine months ago in the pursuit of making it big with your vlog. You are heavy on the pursuit of achieving your goal, to prove the existence of the supernatural to the world at large. Recently, you were sent a file that has footage of something you've never seen. Footage of a man turning into a Wolf. Despite what you've been told your whole life you have in fact discovered that Werewolves, or Wolf Shifters as they sometimes prefer to be called, are very real. I have news, Ms. Grotto, Wolves aren't the only creatures out there. There are many, many more. And they don't like it when humans try to ferret out their secrets. So now, those creatures are hunting you." He stopped at a red light and turned his handsome face to look at her.

"How am I doing for knowing the basics?"

"Um, yeah. Pretty good there, Trench," she muttered.

"Look, I was sent by someone who is trying to get to the bottom of this. You weren't sent that video clip by accident."

"What does that mean?"

"It means I am going to protect you, Bria. If you let me."

Gold eyes flashed, and Bria nodded. For some stupid reason, she believed him.

"Okay, I know I shouldn't, but I believe you. I just really hope you're not a serial killer or something."

"I'm something alright, but I never killed a cereal in my life. Except for a box of *Frosted Flakes*, but that's only because I have an issue with their mascot," he said deadpan.

"Who doesn't like *Tony the Tiger?*"

"Me. He makes Tigers look dumb."

"What? That is ridiculous," she replied as the light turned green and traffic started moving again.

"Doesn't like *Tony the Tiger*," she muttered.

"I meant what I said. I will keep you safe."

"Okay, but I hope I don't end up regretting this."

That earned her something that sounded like a snort and a whisper that sounded something vaguely like *"me too"*.

Bria settled back into the surprisingly comfortable seat. The adrenaline was wearing off, and suddenly she was exhausted. Bria stifled her yawn, but it was no good.

"You can sleep, Bria, we won't get there for another hour or two."

Any lingering doubt she had that maybe the freakishly large male was a serial killer faded as her eyes drooped. Call her a fool if you will, but Bria was so tired after the last few hours of excitement she couldn't seem to stay awake.

Her nose itched for some reason, and she

wondered if she'd gotten any fur from Mrs. Garcia's sweater on her. She sneezed three times in a row, earning her a confused glare from the man.

"Sorry," she mumbled, but he just nodded, handing her a tissue.

"Bless you."

"Thanks."

Then she was out like a light.

CHAPTER FOUR

ISLAND STRIPE PRIDE

ant. Need. Lick. Bite.

What? No!

His human side warred with his animal one. Trench's heart was beating a mile a minute, and he had no idea how to slow it down. Something was wrong.

This woman was a witch or something. It was the only thing that made sense. She was doing something to him, wasn't she? But how? He did not scent magic, just vanilla and orange zest. Reminded him of that clementine cake he'd wanted for his tenth birthday.

Yummy.

What the hell? When did a big ass scary Enforcer start thinking words like that? Was his brain addled by that tiny altercation with those pups? Shit. HE was embarrassed for himself.

Trench never let a female get to him like this. Then again, he'd never been near one who smelled so mouthwateringly delicious, looking like a pinup model from the 50s with curves in all the right places.

Modern women tended to be too skinny for his tastes. Skin and bone with no meat to them. But she had nice wide hips, a heart shaped ass he'd love to nibble, and breasts that could fill even his hands quite nicely. Of course, he'd have to worry about the whole human thing.

Normals were frail, weak. He might hurt her if he ever tried to fuck her. That earned him a snarl from his beast. The Tiger was enraged at the thought of anyone hurting the beautiful female. Least of all him.

Never hurt. Claim. Mine.

What? Shit. When his Tiger started sending him messages in human speech, Trench knew he was in trouble. It happened very rarely. Only in times of extreme danger. So, why now? Then the beast replied, and the answer stunned Trench into swerving on the road. Thank fuck, no one else was around.

Mate, his beast growled.

Shit.

Fuck.

Fucking fuck.

Trench's Tiger had lost his damned mind. He glanced at the adorable female, curled on her side, and softly snoring in the din of the Vette he'd borrowed from Alex, the Pride Beta. The man was gonna shit when he saw what McLeesh's Wolves did to one of his cars.

Oh, well. Couldn't be helped. Trench didn't have another option, since his own new vehicle's delivery was currently delayed. Damn shortage of employees everywhere, it seemed.

No matter. Alex Kensington, like himself and most of the Island Stripe Pride, received more than ample pay, not to mention stock options in their company, *ISP Inc.*, the dividends of which were always more than healthy.

What they did exactly was anyone's guess. *ISP Inc.* had several different interests, including an imports and exports operation which dealt in everything from food products to modern art and priceless antiques.

Living in the city was pricey, and a bit crowded for most Tigers. They worked in groups, but like large amounts of space between even Pride mates.

Manhattan seemed a strange location for their head-quarters, but like the jungles where their wild cousins roamed, the Big Apple was a concrete wilderness. It provided enough entertainment for even a big Cat to remain interested.

Not an easy feat, Trench knew from experience. New York had a lot of limelight and glitter, and beneath that was enough grime and dirt for the sometimes rough and tumble world of Shifters. But even the wildest of men and beasts needed something soft once in a while.

That was where the Fates came in. Some Shifters were content with lukewarm meetings and casual encounters. Others believed in something greater than themselves. He'd never thought about it much. Had considered he was for a life alone, after all, he was a killer. Trained in combat, he knew forty seven ways to kill someone before the target even knew what was happening.

Trench was quick to react. His physical prowess was his strength, and his dominant beast demanded he respond to all threats the same way. Kill or be killed. That was the life of an Enforcer. He was an elite warrior even among Shifters. How could he possibly have a mate?

True, the same was said for Dean Romero and

Alex Kensington. But they were both now happily mated with cubs too. Trench had seen the changes in his Neta and their Pride Beta when both men, once the most eligible bachelors in the Pride, looked upon their mates.

He'd assumed having a mate would make a Shifter weak, forcing him to change focus. But their respective women had not hurt them in any way. In fact, they'd only served to make the two Tigers Trench admired the most ever fiercer.

He turned to steal a glance at Bria. She was sleeping peacefully, completely trusting in him, a total stranger, to care for her. Maybe she was crazy? He wondered. But again his Tiger growled. No one would speak ill of her in the animal's presence. Not even him.

Mine.

The truth was hard to swallow. It had simply never occurred to Trench that he might have a mate. There were other ways to procreate, for sure. Tiger only, or interspecies, depending on one's preference, dating services were available. There were also Pride or Pack mixers, where couples were invited to meet and copulate for the purpose of having cubs.

Straightforward and simple. The parents of any resulting offspring would work out visitation terms without having to deal with messy relationship entanglements, and the always eventual divorce. At least, that was what his mother said. His own parents had taken part in such an arrangement. They'd met at a retreat for adults looking for prospective partners to father/bear their young.

"We were two consenting adults who wanted to have a cub without the mess," was how his father had always described it.

Trench never thought it was weird until now. Sitting in the small vehicle, windows rolled up in deference to her humanity and the chilly night air, he couldn't help but breathe in her fragrance. The beast wanted to roll around in it, but since he had to drive, Trench decided to sort through each nuance of her scent.

The activity calmed him, gave him something to look forward to. From where he sat, his supernaturally enhanced olfactory senses picked up on the subtle notes of vanilla orchids, sweet citrus bursts, and heady musk that made his Tiger want to purr. Images of the curvy beauty in the middle of his king sized bed filled his brain at the same time she moaned softly in her sleep. The sound so intoxicatingly tempting, Trench almost swerved right into a ditch.

Fuck.

He needed to get a hold of himself. But how was he supposed to do that? His inner Cat scratched against his skin, wanting him to claim the slumbering female, but his human mind knew better. No woman would appreciate being bitten in the middle of a car ride.

Duh.

For one thing, it would hurt. For another, there was a little something called consent. Now, call him crazy, but Trench would really like to have that before he sunk his teeth, or any other part of him for that matter, into the gorgeous creature.

Yeah, there was that, he mused.

Then again, maybe his Tiger's way wasn't all that bad. The animal part of his dual nature had suggested Trench pull over, then he could start licking the lovely little human until she woke up.

Then maybe, just maybe, he would get to keep on licking her, *and licking her,* until she submitted to him. Her vanilla citrus scent already had his mouth watering. He could hardly wait to learn if she tasted just as sweet.

Kiss, lick, nibble. Oooh, yes.

He was drooling just thinking about making her come on his tongue, and his fingers, then his cock.

Driving with a hard on in the close confines of the Corvette was worth it if just so he could fantasize about her. Fuck, but would it ever happen? Would Trench be able to lay his claim on the sweet female?

Grrr. Fuck yes, his animal insisted.

We could do that, his human side agreed.

But only after she says yes.

Fine. Convince her then, the Tiger conceded with a hungry growl.

Concentrate, he scolded himself. Bad enough he was horny like a teenager just being near her. His fucking, or not fucking to put it more accurately, cock was already threatening to punch straight through the thick denim jeans he wore. But he ignored it. He had to. She was a normal, and she was in trouble from his kind.

Grrr.

His Tiger did not like the reminder. Regardless of whatever actions got her into this, no human deserved to be targeted by a Pack of disloyal Were-wolves. He would protect her now. No matter the cost.

Trench Tora was very good at his job. Before he became an Enforcer for the Island Stripe Pride, he was a soldier. Trained to kill, and really fucking good at it, he'd been recruited to a special ops team made up of mainly Shifters. His reputation preceded him. Reaching the ears of Dean Romero himself. The Neta had welcomed the prodigal Tiger home with open arms and a shiny new position in the Pride. As an Enforcer, Trench's job was to protect the Pride.

He was sanctioned by both Neta and Nari, the Neta's mate, to perform his duties by any means necessary. Trench was really good at that part. So yeah, he would protect the female at any costs.

Maybe, if he were lucky, Trench could convince the sweet-smelling woman that she was made for him. Of course, any impending mating needed to wait until he settled this thing with the Wolves and the Council. In the meantime, he'd carry her back to his den, *er*, hunting cabin in the woods to lie low for a bit.

Maybe the forced time together would be good. He could wax poetic on his good points. Like he could tell her about how he broke all the company records for stealth, speed, and most lethal hand to hand combat. Hmm. Or maybe she'd be fucking scared shitless of him if he told her that shit.

Trench's brows furrowed. What else was there? He wasn't what he'd call a very deep person. He liked peace and quiet. Sometimes, he liked to climb to a sturdy branch and take naps in the morning sun.

Oooh, and he liked stalking his prey. But he never toyed with them. Well, not too much, anyway.

Fuck.

This was so not helping. He'd never doubted himself before. How could one woman make him so damn unsure of himself?

It did not matter. Now that she was in his sights, there was only one thing to do. The Tiger was going to claim his mate. There was no other option for him if he wanted to go on living, and Trench had no desire to end his time on the earth. Not yet anyway.

Not when he'd finally found her. Yep. No ifs, ands or buts about it. Trench Tora needed Bria Grotto to be his.

Rooaaarrrrr!

CHAPTER FIVE

ISLAND STRIPE PRIDE

Left, right, left right.

Bria rocked from side to side in a steady rhythm that reminded her of her grandfather's old sailboat. He'd had a summer down in the Florida Keys, and she'd loved to visit when she was a kid. But that had been years ago. Something rumbled beneath her, like a giant motor and she tried to rack her brain for where she was but came up empty.

It was no good. Time to wakey…

"When did we board a boat?" Bria asked and blinked herself awake.

She didn't smell the ocean, but that same, steady, side to side rocking had to be caused by one seaworthy vessel or another. By the time she opened her eyes, she realized her error. She wasn't on a boat, and the hard, warm bed cushioning her body was, in fact, a man.

It was him. Her stranger. The man who rescued her from the big bad, *er*, Wolves. Trench Tora in the flesh.

And what nice, firm flesh it was, she thought, feeling her cheeks heat at the errant thought.

"Ooh!"

Bria gasped, almost upending herself. Good thing he had a firm hold of her with one arm across her back and the other beneath her knees. She tightened her arms around his neck, afraid she'd break something falling from that ridiculous height. How tall was he, anyway?"

"Six feet, eight inches," he replied.

Crap. She'd asked that aloud.

"My cabin's a mile and a half into the woods from the access road," he said in a pleasantly deep voice that had shivers racing across her skin.

"Oh?"

"Yep. We're almost there."

"You've been carrying me for a mile and a half?" she asked astounded.

"Almost a mile and a half," he corrected.

Holy crap. That was not okay. Bria was not a

small girl. Well, she was short, but height was the only thing small about her.

Bria was what polite folks called *pleasantly plump,* and what her older brother affectionately called *cute, but chubby*. What could she say? She liked food.

In all honesty, she could probably afford to lose weight, but she'd been on every fad diet that had passed through all the talk shows, and those cheap women's magazines you found at the checkout line at the supermarket, since high school. The result was always the same.

In self-defense, she'd learned to love her curves. And she had plenty of them. Even her curves had curves. No matter what she'd tried, there was just no getting rid of the soft belly, big breasts, and thick thighs.

Genetics was real, people, and her name wasn't the only thing she'd gotten from her Italian paternal grandmother. Apparently, the first Bria Grotto had an ass that wouldn't quit when she'd been younger. Something her granddaughter was keenly aware of since it bumped against Trench's rock hard abdomen with every step he took.

She couldn't believe he walked for a mile and a half *carrying her*. Did she mention that already? That he was still carrying her?

Gulp.

That was so hot.

"Um, I can walk---"

"Quicker this way," he murmured.

She had to admit, he wasn't wrong. His long legs plowed through the budding foliage of the forest as easily as a hot knife through butter. Just as quickly, too. She'd bet she'd need to take three steps for one of his. Oh well, she might as well let him have at it.

Was it wrong she was enjoying the ride?

Bria rarely got the chance to feel so dainty and small. And this guy was a veritable giant. Good looking too. Bria was a fan of beauty. She loved attending museums and reading books. Especially those juicy fun romance novels she digested chapter by chapter.

Trench Tora was seriously beautiful. She took stock of all the tanned skin revealed at the low V of his shirt, the bulging biceps that strained the material, and the pecs and abs that protected her like a heated wall. His chiseled jaw, hard mouth, and gold eyes were stunning. The man could be a model.

He must have to fight them off with a stick, she mused and studied his face with an appreciative eye. She felt him slow down, that gorgeous face turning to her.

"Something wrong?" he asked, with one perfectly arched eyebrow raised inquisitively.

"Hmm? Why do you ask?"

"You're staring," he said, seemingly concerned.

"Am I? Sorry, you're just really good looking," she said, opting for honesty.

"What?" he asked, and she thought she heard a chuckle.

"You heard me," she repeated, rolling her eyes. "Anyway," Bria continued. Just cause he was handsome, didn't mean she had to fan his ego. "Nothing is wrong. I just, well, I mean you told me your name, but I don't know anything about you."

"Um, well, aside from my good looks and impressive walking skills, you mean?" he joked.

"Oh, come on. I wasn't that bad."

"You were, but I appreciate it, Bria. Um, we're here," he said, breaking their previously prolonged eye contact.

He climbed a set of wooden steps that led to a narrow porch. Trench swallowed, allowing Bria to slide down his body till her feet touched the step. There was no ick factor at all.

In fact, he was disappointingly appropriate about the entire thing. Sigh. She lamented the wasted opportunity, giving him a small, somewhat embarrassed smile. Bria was, after all, heavy for a woman. But then, the man was not even breaking a sweat.

Curious.

"Let me get the door," he murmured.

He slid past her carefully, probably so he didn't knock her down. The staircase was narrow as well. She assumed the small patio just ended there, but curiosity had gotten the better of her, and she'd walked the few steps to the edge.

Mouth agape, Bria took in the rest of what was actually an immense wrap-around porch. From the front, the cabin was small and unassuming, but the back was positively luxurious. A wooden deck expanded a few dozen feet in every direction. It held a large firepit shaped like a roaring tiger's mouth and beautiful Adirondack chairs.

Everything was lacquered to protect against the elements, but none of that red or brown paint. This was all clear coated, allowing for the beauty of the wood to shine through.

It was breathtaking. For one fanciful moment, Bria wondered how it would look in the snow. Or even better, in the middle of springtime with the promise of summer on the breeze. Bria would love to sit in one of those gorgeous chairs with an afghan over her legs and the morning sun shining down while she drank fresh brewed coffee from her favorite mug, an open book on her lap.

"You coming in?"

"What? Yes," she replied, bringing herself back to reality.

She turned towards where the big man waited, just watching her with that unwavering stare. Bria didn't know how long she'd been standing, simply staring, but his voice didn't startle her. That meant he must have been there just as long. It was likely then that she'd been aware of his presence.

An intuitive person, she believed in signs. She depended on her inner alarm system, the one that set off warning bells inside of her, alerting her to times of danger.

Like when those goons had tried to pounce on her, and she knew instinctively that she had to scram. That trusty system of hers had stayed blissfully quiet with Trench near.

And wasn't that interesting? There was just something about Trench Tora that made her feel safe. Foolish? Maybe. But she didn't think so. Bria had always been a big believer in the innate goodness of people.

Also, there was that one other little quirk she'd inherited from her grandmother, besides the fat ass and her name. Of course, her mother and father were not too keen on it, but Bria was a stouthearted believer in her advanced female intuition.

Grandma had called it *knowing*. She'd told Bria that sometimes a Grotto woman simply knew things that no one else would or could. Maybe it was from just paying attention. Or maybe she was truly blessed by the saints, as Nonna seemed to think. Raised Catholic, she knew all about miracles and divine intervention.

Still, Bria was wise enough to know there were more things in the universe than a person could possibly imagine. She would be foolish to believe otherwise. But anyway, back to the matter at hand.

"Trench?"

"Yeah," he replied, his unblinking gold stare kept her rooted to the spot.

"Would you come here a sec?"

"I'm right here, Bria."

"I know, but would you mind," she said, biting her lip.

It was presumptuous of her, but she placed her hands on either side of his gorgeous face and tugged him down to eye level. The fact that he went willingly was telling. His skin felt equally rough and smooth. How he managed that, she couldn't hazard a guess. He was drop dead gorgeous though, devastatingly so this close.

Bria pushed everything else away. Removing herself from the very real awareness of her intense attraction to him, his ridiculously delicious scent, *like candy apples and sunflowers,* and the fact he was perhaps the most handsome man she'd ever seen let alone touched, Bria refocused.

"I'm here," he said, closer now than before.

"Shhh," she replied.

She inhaled a deep breath, taking in the scent of the woods and his own special fragrance with that gulp of breath. Concentrating solely on her *knowing* skills, Bria allowed the whole entire world to just fade away while she took him in.

"What are you doing?" he whispered.

"Making sure I can trust you," she whispered back.

Trench Tora, she thought his name, saw it written out in fiery bold letters in her mind. The man was fierce, but she didn't need any intuition to tell her that. Loyal? Yes.

There was darkness in him, but it was too small to consider a threat. He could be violent and lethal, but that was what made him a good protector. No, what she saw was his goodness. And that mattered the most.

Trench was good. Very, very good. Especially deep down inside where it counted the most. He was a good man. Strong, honest, dependable, and sweet. She saw his sweetness buried beneath the rest, as if he were hiding it from the world. And didn't that make her want to dig it out? Yes. It really did.

"Okay," she said, making her mind to stay put.

"Okay?"

"Yep," she replied, moving past him to get inside the cabin.

"Bria? What the hell just happened?" Trench asked.

His voice was slightly louder, and he was seemingly confused. She watched the big man run a hand over his head and Bria noted the unusual colors. Having turned on the porch light when they'd arrived, she now saw he had hints of red in the predominantly brown locks. But stranger, were the thick black streaks throughout.

Somehow, it worked on him. Trench's hair was thick and impossibly glossy. Her fingers itched to test its softness, and she wondered if he would let her.

Once again, she had to work to stay focused on

the topic, though. Pushing away all inappropriate thoughts of touching the big man. He'd rescued her, and she didn't think it wise to push her luck.

"Can't you tell me what all that was?"

"Oh, you mean that thing I did a moment ago?" she asked.

"Yes," he replied patiently. *"That."*

"Like I said, I was just making sure you were trustworthy."

"Trustworthy? And looking at my face told you I was?"

"Yep."

"But you don't know me."

"Don't have to know you to know you're a good man," she said easily.

"How can you possibly know I'm a good man from that?"

"Well, are you?" she asked, unwilling to share her little quirk just yet.

"I guess that depends on who you ask," he answered.

She could tell it was as forthright a comment as she was going to get out of him. He was tense and deep in thought. Bria didn't like that. Not one bit. So, she headed for the clearest path to be happy, and that was to be honest.

"Am I safe with you?" she stopped and asked him point blank.

"What?"

"Am. I. Safe."

Bria believed in being frank and getting to the heart of things quickly. Life was too short for beating around the bush. She noticed a twitch at the corner of Trench's straight mouth. Like he was fighting a grin. She had to admit that was something she'd love to see. Later maybe. When he trusted her a little bit more, then she'd make him collapse into bales of laughter.

"You are safer with me than anywhere else in the entire world, Bria Grotto," Trench stated with absolute certainty.

"There," she replied, nodding. "I told you."

Then she walked inside his cabin, and her jaw hit the floor.

WOWZA.

CHAPTER SIX

ISLAND STRIPE PRIDE

"Holy cow," Bria whispered reverently.

Trench had to admit his chest swelled with pride at the way she was looking at his cabin. After all, he had built the damn thing with his own hands. On nights and weekends over the course of the last two years.

"Is everything okay?" he asked, just to make sure.

"Better than okay, Trench. This is beautiful," she replied.

Trench watched the unusual female walk around his cabin. He found himself watching her reactions, saving them for later investigation in the vault that was his mind.

Her impossibly dark brown eyes widened as she ran her soft, warm hands across his furniture, marveling at every little thing. He knew her hands were both soft and warm because she'd touched him only moments ago and he still felt the heat of them on his cheeks. They felt really good on his skin.

Grrr.

His Tiger chuffed, the animal thrilled that his mate had willingly touched him. He had to admit he was shocked, and not much surprised him anymore. Trench had seen and done things that would cause the hair to go white on even the most stouthearted of Shifters. Most people gave him a wide berth, but not her. This tiny normal had announced that she trusted him after he pretty much kidnapped her from outside her apartment after kicking some Were-wolves' asses.

Just about every positive emotion he'd ever heard, most a foreign experience for him, flitted through him as he studied the lovely female. She was like a curious kitten, he thought as pride, passion, protective instincts, possession, and a deep and undeniable warmth filled him.

Along with the need to keep her safe, his desire for her rose with every passing minute. How did the Fates know she would be the one for him? They couldn't be more different, but damn, how she called out to him. His soul ached to be near her, and he wondered if she felt any attraction on some level for him as well.

The way her gaze kept coming back to him told him she did. But he wasn't sure. And the uncertainty was killing him.

Bria was asking him questions about the cabin. But Trench had been so busy staring at her delectable bottom as she bent over to stare at the details on the carved mantel- *the one he'd built himself*, he'd missed her inquiry.

"I said, is this the work of a local artist?"

"Huh? Oh, um, sort of," he replied, scratching the back of his neck.

"Name?"

"Uh, Trench Tora?" he replied, but it came out more question than statement.

"You did not!"

"Yes, I did."

"Wow, you really are an artist, then. But how did you make it, so it was part of the wall?"

"Well, I did that intentionally when I built that side---"

"Shut the fuck up, you did not build this cabin!" she screeched, and now he was really confused.

Should he answer? Deny? What?

"Well?" she asked.

Her brown eyes were bright with what he determined to be happiness. Thank fuck. Otherwise, he never would have answered her.

"Yeah. This is my cabin. I built it from the ground up."

"Omg, marry me?" she teased.

Or at least, he assumed she was teasing. Deep down, though, he wanted to scream YES. Was it too soon? Probably. Fuck.

"How long did it take? Was it just you?"

"About two years, cause of work, and I had a few friends help with some of it," he explained.

Trench wasn't one to brag, and he hated the spotlight. Unlike Lion males, Tigers were innately solitary beasts. He never sought out attention for any reason. But he liked hers. Liked that she appreciated the things he could do with his hands. And there was so much more he could do other than carve things.

Want to show her, his beast pushed the thought into his head, and he struggled for control.

It was highly unusual for Trench to lose control of his inner Tiger. Too dangerous for anyone near him, truth be told. He'd learned to master his beast when he'd been little more than a cub. Something his mother had insisted on.

His father had been keen to have offspring, but the old man was never around much during those formative years. When it became evident his son was powerful, he'd shipped him off to military school. Trench enrolled in the service and was soon scooped up by a top secret Shifter ops team. After his stint in the military, he'd messed around with security firms, then he came back home to New York as an Enforcer for the Pride.

Mother was proud, but he couldn't help but think he'd disappointed her. She was an academic, a guest lecturer at Columbia University. Cela Trench had always been a firm believer in brain over brawn. Not that her son was an idiot. He held advanced degrees in science and mathematics.

"Oh my, look at all these books!"

Bria grinned at him, and his heart slammed against his ribs. She was astonishingly adorable. Especially when that dimple next to her mouth peeked out.

"Have you read all these?"

Unable to speak yet, Trench nodded. Fuck. All his experience and education were useless to him in the face of the prettiest damn woman he'd ever seen. In all his years, he'd never been flummoxed by a smile.

But this wasn't any smile. This was his future mate's smile.

But was he worthy? Frowning, Trench set about locking the door, securing the windows, and setting the advanced alarm system before he started the fireplace.

"Oh, that's nice," she said, moving closer to the flames. "You have been so awesome, and I hate to ask this, but---"

Just then, her stomach rumbled, and Trench could have kicked himself. What kind of prospective mate was he if he didn't remember to feed his mate?

"Shit. You're hungry. Right, I'm on it," he replied, and practically tripped over himself getting to the kitchen.

Uh oh. He really needed to go shopping. Mostly, Trench kept freeze dried military rations around. It made sense, after all, he'd usually just hunt in his fur if he wanted fresh meat. But he didn't think she would appreciate him turning into his half ton Tiger in the living room. Even if it was built specifically with that in mind.

Trench was still digging through the cabinets when Bria joined him. He didn't have to hear her to know she was there. Her warm vanilla and citrus fragrance had already reached his nostrils, making him dizzy with hunger. And not for anything he had in his cabinets.

"Don't go out of your way," she said, breaking the silence. "I think I have a granola bar in my bag."

The Tiger in him chuffed. But her observation at least had his boner going back to half-mast. He doubted he would ever be completely flaccid in her presence. And there it went back to hard again. Fuck.

"Um, well, let's see," he mumbled. He really needed to stop thinking about his dick around her. "I have a box of spaghetti, some sea salt, a can of plum shaped tomatoes, peas, a jar of minced garlic, and a bottle of olive oil."

Trench waved the half used bottle and tried to not be embarrassed. Fuck, he never recalled feeling so absolutely useless in front of a woman. Couldn't he just kill something for her? That would be easier.

"I can work with that," Bria grinned, grabbing the goods and moving to the stove.

He was so stunned, he let her. In fact, he stood like an idiot while Bria rummaged for a pot in the cabinets. She handed one to him with that sexy little grin on her face, the one that brought out her dimple, and fuck, there he went again.

Boing!

"Here," she said. "Fill this with water and add some sea salt. Do you have a saucepan?"

"Sure. What else do you need?"

"How about a knife, can opener, and cutting board?"

"Yeah, I can do that," he muttered, and dug through his kitchen for everything she might need.

Together, they chopped, sauteed, boiled, and eventually had the makings of a pretty damn decent meal. One of the best he'd ever had, truth be told.

"I never had peas in my pasta before," he said around a mouthful of the most amazing spaghetti ever known to human or Shifter.

"No? My dad's family is Southern Italian. He'd put peas in everything if he could," Bria explained with laughter in her voice.

He loved that about her. She found the best in every situation and was always laughing or smiling. But not because she was an idiot. Far from it.

Trench thought most people were idiots. Their voices and laughter grated on his nerves. But he liked the noises she made, and the sound of her chatter. Even those tiny little snorts at the end of her laugh. Cute as fuck, each one of them.

Surprise filled him as the minutes ticked by. Not only was he blown away by how delicious the food tasted, but by the fact he was truly enjoying her company. Bria Grotto was an unknown element. She was so different from everyone he knew, certainly the women in his life.

Female Shifters were even meaner than the males, in his experience. His mother, God love her, was always good to him, but she was never very openly affectionate. Not even with her only son.

Those he dated were much the same. Using sex to scratch a biological itch, without any emotional entanglements. It had worked for him in the past, but he'd never felt anything after wards. It was always just as clinical and necessary as washing his hands before eating or brushing his teeth.

One look at Bria, especially with that tiny speck of sauce on her chin, and he just knew that sex with her would be soul-crushingly deep and life-altering. For the first time in his life, Trench was scared.

Did he really deserve a mate? Was he good enough for this sweet normal who blindly put her life in his hands but only after she tested him with her inner alarm test thingy?

Crazy, beautiful, maddening little kitten.

Yessss. Oursss, the Tiger hissed, pushing the man towards the woman.

"I'll get the dishes." Trench stood up once they'd

finished everything in the pot along with the half a bag of chocolate chips he'd had in the cupboard for dessert.

"Mind if I explore?" Bria asked.

"Knock yourself out," he replied easily.

He needed a minute to compose himself and gather his thoughts. Once the dishwasher was loaded and everything was wiped down, he returned to the living room. Bria was on the floor with the bag he'd carried inside the cabin with her just a little while ago. She had her laptop open and was frowning at the screen.

"You won't get any internet out here," he commented.

"I know. But I thought you should see why tonight happened."

Trench nodded and moved closer to her. He was curious what she was going to say, but unhappy that it was causing her stress. He could tell she was struggling with something.

"I received an email the other day with a video clip proving something I had been searching for my whole life," she started.

"Bria, you don't have to," he told her.

"I know, but I think I need to. Now, this is going to sound dumb, and you might even think I'm crazy," Bria continued, raising a hand when he would have interrupted.

"You see, I run a vlog, *Lost and Found: Proof of the Supernatural in the City*. And well, I have been looking for proof of paranormal activity. I think this is it," she said quietly, turning the screen towards him.

Trench watched the video, careful to hide his reactions. It was grainy, true. But it was also footage of an actual Wolf Shifter changing into his animal form in an alley behind the popular *Stripe Club* which was owned and operated by one of the few Tigers not affiliated with any Pride in the Big Apple.

"I also know based on the altercation you had with the three goons who attacked me outside my apartment building that you are one of them. Now, I am not going to hurt you, Trench, but I have to know. Am I right?"

Trench wasn't sure he heard her correctly. Was this sweet innocent telling him she had proof of the supernatural and was she also admitting she believed he was one of them? A fucking dog? His Tiger was mildly insulted. But that was beside the fucking point.

His Pride leader was temporarily in charge of the SCNYC, and that meant he was working for them. Trench had been on these kinds of missions before, where he had to investigate a normal who knew too much. He knew what happened if said normal was unrelated, as in *not mated*, to a Shifter.

Keeping the Shifter secret was imperative to their survival as a species. As an Enforcer, it was his job to guard and protect it. But as a man, as a Tiger male sitting with his potential mate, Trench was at an impasse.

One look into her big brown, trusting eyes, and he knew he could not lie. He wouldn't. Never to her.

"Yes," he said, gauging her reaction.

Surprisingly, the female seemed unmoved. She just slid the computer back towards her and closed it, placing it back inside her bag. A minute passed, then another. He just sat there, waiting for her to find her voice. Trench was not what he would call particularly patient, but he'd been known to sit unmoving and wait for his prey for hours, sometimes days, while on a mission.

This was pretty much the same. Only this time, Trench was emotionally invested in the outcome. Whatever happened, he wanted Bria safe and happy. Wasn't that odd? Certainly was unusual for him anyway.

"When you were fighting those guys, your eyes,"

she said, clearing her throat. "They changed. That's how I knew. So, um, can I see it."

"What?" he asked, certain he'd misheard her.

"Your Wolf?"

"I am not a Wolf!" he practically shouted.

"But you said---"

"I think we need to clear some things up." He began, standing up and pacing.

Fuck. Was he really going to do this?

"Trench, just be honest with me."

"I am, Bria. But promise you won't scream?"

She waited a beat. Then Bria nodded, and Trench took her for her word. His Tiger burst forth, shredding his clothing, and roared into existence as he had a thousand times before.

"Holy shit! T-TIGER!"

CHAPTER SEVEN

ISLAND STRIPE PRIDE

"Trench, just be honest with me."

"I am, Bria. But promise you won't scream?"

Well, shit.

She'd really, really, *really* intended to keep that promise. But how was she supposed to anticipate what happened next? She was a simple Jersey girl from Paramus, known for its shopping malls! Her infatuation with all things supernatural might have started as a kid reading those *Goosebumps* books by R.L. Stein, but up until she received that video, Bria had had zero experience with anything supernatural.

Not firsthand, anyway. No UFO lights or mysterious growling from the shadows. No remnants of fairy dust or gory ghosts lurking in her bedroom.

Her intuition, or *knowing* as Grandma Grotto called it, was as close to it as she'd ever gotten. And that was spooky enough.

This was completely out of her experience. One second, a sexy strapping Trench was staring at her with his beautiful golden eyes, and the next, *bam*, he was all furry and stripey. And big. Did she mention he was really fucking big?

So, um, yeah… Bria fucking screamed.

Like a little girl.

She screamed, raising her hand, pointing at the enormous furry beast.

"Holy shit! T-TIGER!"

Okay, so it was not her finest moment. She'd barely had time to come down from the coffee table she'd foolishly jumped on, *like that was going to save her,* when he was back in his skin.

Only naked. Like *naked naked.*

Totally fucking naked.

Gulp.

Bria had seen nude men before, but this guy was a work of art. And… he was fucking huge. Trench's eyes were on her face, arms raised wide as if approaching a frightened animal, and did she mention he was still naked?

"Easy. I am not going to hurt you, Bria."

"I bet you say that to all the girls before you eat them! OHMYGAHD!"

Heart pounding, her eyesight grew blurry. Bria was having a panic attack. She turned to Trench, still pissed, but what choice did she have?

"You better catch me, dammit!"

Then everything went black.

* * *

Sometime later…

Bria blinked her eyes. She was in a huge bed with a fluffy soft blanket. Definitely not hers. Where the heck was she?

Then it all came back, rushing into her brain. She was nearly drowning in the impossibility of it all. Trench, the dirty rat, *er*, cat, actually, was sleeping sitting up in a chair beside the bed.

Aww. That was kind of nice, actually. He'd given up his bed for her. But why? Did he want his snack comfy before he ate it? She spied a glass of water beside her and risked a small sip. It wasn't poisoned, so she took another. Then, she glared at the softly snoring man, and tossed the cold contents right at him.

He woke up with a roar and Bria jumped on the

bed, startled.

"What the fu---" he blinked, wiping his face off and calming the second he saw her.

"Bria? Are you okay?"

"Am I okay," she growled, pissed off. "You lied, you *lying liar*."

"Uh..." Trench stood there, dripping wet and looking ridiculously cute for someone who was drooling a moment ago.

"How did I lie?" he asked.

"You are not a Wolf," she said, shaking her head.

"I never said I was a Wolf. You assumed I was a Wolf. I am a Shifter though, a Tiger Shifter."

"I know! You showed me, remember?" she shouted, seriously annoyed.

Did he think she was a fucking idiot? Bria had been to the Bronx Zoo a time or twelve. She knew Tigers when she saw one. Okay, so she'd never seen a man turn into a Tiger, but so what?

"Bria, let's have some coffee, okay? Then we can talk about this."

"Coffee, you say?"

She sniffed, nodding her head. She could go for some coffee.

"Yeah. Coffee and breakfast! I'll make you whatever you want, well, within reason," he muttered.

"Fine, but I need a shower first."

"Right through there. I brought your bag up too," he replied, showing her where everything was before he left the room.

Twenty minutes later, with her teeth brushed, hair shampooed and combed, and smelling fresh like the Dove soap he had in his luxurious bathroom, Bria joined Trench downstairs. He looked freshly showered as well, and she figured he must have a second bathroom somewhere.

"Outside shower, for when I come back muddy and stuff," he muttered, responding to her confusion.

"Okay," she replied. "Coffee?"

She'd smelled the rich, tempting fragrance of freshly brewed coffee from upstairs. Now she was the one drooling.

"I only have powdered creamer, apologies," he said, handing her some packets.

"It's fine," she replied quietly.

"Look, I want to---" he started, but she needed to get this off her chest first.

"Please, let me apologize. I am so embarrassed by my outburst. This is all so out of my league. Wolves, Tigers, Shifters, and then you running in, and rescuing me, and then this place. And you're so gorgeous, and considerate, and you make me feel safe. You gave me your bed, and then I go and scream at you like a crazy person---"

"First of all, you have every right to be discombobulated by all of this," he began.

"Did you just use discombobulated in a sentence?"

"Um, yeah," he paused, but she had nothing else to add. So, he continued.

"Anyway, um, none of this is your fault, Bria. You just happened to get an email that is highly sensitive to our people. I know, you didn't know what you were looking at or the ramifications, but the fact is, there are people after you now. I promise I will help you, keep you safe. And I didn't mean to scare you. I just thought you should see my Cat," he finished, rubbing a hand over his head.

He seemed to do that a lot when he was thinking. Bria bit her lip. It was a lot of information, and she had the feeling he'd never said so much at one time to one person.

"Sorry, I don't usually talk to, well, anyone," he murmured. "But I do want to say something."

"What?"

"I think you're gorgeous too," he stated matter-of-factly.

Before she could even start to contemplate that, Bria jumped up, nearly knocking over her coffee. Werewolves were real. Weretigers were real. She had proof. He was proof.

"Ohmygahd!" Bria blurted. "I'm gonna be famous! My vlog is gonna blow up. YOU are proof of everything!"

But even before she saw him shaking his head, hands raised in alarm, Bria knew that was not going to happen. How could it? These creatures were obviously hiding for a reason. And wouldn't it be interesting to find out? Even if only for herself— *hell yes, it would!*

"No, Bria, you can't do that," he said, shaking his head.

"Hmm? What now?"

"You see, the Shifter world must remain secret. You can't tell anyone else. There are powerful Shifters who know you have that video, and they are already hunting you. I am going to keep you safe, but we need to delete that video."

"Wait. Slow down," she said, trying to not look at his manly torso just sitting there in the daylight.

Did he even own a shirt? How was a girl supposed to think with all those tanned muscles?

And why the hell was he tanned? It wasn't even beach weather yet.

"Hey, my face is here," he said, and she could hear the smile in his voice.

"Sorry," she murmured, squeezing her eyes shut.

"I don't mind you looking at me, Bria, if it brings you pleasure. Hell, you can look, touch, anything you want," he said, and the man purred.

Honest to God *purred*. Bria swooned. Her insides melted. Liquid pooled between her legs, and a fierce pang of arousal spiked in her blood. Bria wasn't a nun, for fuck's sake. She had needs. And getting it on with this huge, smexy Tiger man was like number one in her list of things she needed.

Like now.

"Trench, I'm so sorry. You must think I am a total nut job. Here you've been nothing but nice to me, saving me from those guys, bringing me here, feeding me, letting me sleep in your bed, explaining your secret to me, and I'm like panting after you like some sex starved maniac," she blurted out in one extremely long winded sentence.

"You're not panting. But with some work, I think I can change that," he pointed out, unhelpfully.

"Wait. Are you flirting with me? We've got some pretty serious things to discuss, and here I am beating myself up over being all inappropriate, but---"

She gulped.

"But, um---"

"What?" he asked, grinning again.

"I was wondering if, maybe, um, you kinda sorta like it when I think inappropriately about you? *Mebbe?*"

Then he stood, trapping her against the table. All six feet, eight inches of Trench Tora was standing in front of her like God's gift to Bria, and all she could do was look at his eyes.

Those incredible eyes of his were burning bright, just like the tiger in the poem by William Blake. Two hundred years later, and the man's accurate description wowed Bria in that small cabin somewhere in the woods in upstate New York.

Trench's eyes did indeed burn. Not like embers or sparklers this time, but like the flames of a blazing inferno.

Dangerous. Mysterious. Sexy as sin.

Bria wasn't afraid of him or his beast, but she was tempted. Very much so.

"Well?"

"Well, to answer your question, I like *you*, Bria

Grotto. And yes, I would very much like to get inappropriate with you."

"Oh," she replied, placing her hands tentatively on his hot skin.

She pushed away from the dining table, careful not to jar the coffee. Trench moved willingly, thrilling her with his pliability.

Her pulse was racing. Bria never did things like this. Maybe it was her female intuition thing, but she'd never felt this way about anyone else. Only him.

So, she went with her gut and plastered herself to the man. Thank fuck, she thought as his arms came around her. Next, Trench's hard line of a mouth sealed over hers in a kiss that was impossibly soft, and filled with passion. It was so damn sweet, it would have made even an angel weep.

But Bria wasn't an angel. She didn't weep. Instead, she decided to grab this opportunity by the hand. Like those cavalier poets that came before Blake, Bria seized the moment.

Carpe Diem, she thought with a healthy addition of *o captain, my captain*. Fuck, that was a good movie.

Focus, Bria.

Fuck. Trench was leaning down, larger than life and sexier than any man should ever be allowed to be. His sunflower scent filled her nostrils, and she could practically taste his heat.

"I want you," she whispered.

"Mine," he replied, surprising her with the thrill of excitement that flooded her at the barely intelligible word.

Then he kissed her. Softly first, slowly, teasing her lips into parting. He slid his tongue between them, exploring her mouth. She allowed it, hell, she'd beg for it if he'd dared stop, so entranced she was by his sensual touch and the purring noise coming from his chest.

Then the kiss turned urgent, and his arms wrapped around her body. Bria moaned, holding on, clutching his shoulders as he lifted her and carried her to the living room. A fire was already stoked in the beautiful fireplace. Appropriate for the chilly spring morning.

He took them both down to the soft rug, expertly, gently. Taking the brunt of the fall, Bria was sprawled atop him, grateful she'd donned her soft leggings and loose tank top for coffee. They'd be easy to remove, she thought wickedly.

Trench kissed her like he was starving, and he couldn't get enough. Bria had never felt such a ferocious desire, and she loved it. Her body was on fire for him. Her heart too.

Nails bit into his biceps. Maybe it was the close call she'd had earlier, her brush with violence and possible death, but she didn't think so. It was simply him.

Being near him, she felt things she'd never thought possible. He peeled away her clothing layer by layer, kissing and touching, praising her as he revealed her secrets inch by inch.

Bria was a big girl, often shy and sometimes insecure, but his words were from his heart. She felt his honesty. Believed he thought she was beautiful, and in turn, she felt like she was. To him, in that moment, and what else mattered?

"You *are* beautiful, kitten," Trench said, the steel in his voice daring her to disagree.

Why would she? He nodded, satisfied with her acquiescence, and went back to exploring her. Bria was not passive, she kissed and touched her fill too. But he was overwhelming her with his talented hands and most dexterous tongue.

"Oh Trench," she moaned as his hot hands stripped her of her top.

He growled, looking his fill before lowering his head to kiss her heavy breasts. She was swollen with need, and fuck, it felt so good when he sucked and nibbled her there. Oooh, there. Trench wasn't finished though, thank fuck.

He ran his hands over her soft belly, down to the apex of her thighs. Coasting his fingers across her damp panties, she wiggled, trying to tempt him closer. Fuck, she didn't want to wait. She wanted him to touch her. To make her feel good. She wanted him to make her come.

"Trench!" Bria moaned his name, impatient and needy.

"What is it, kitten?"

"Please," she begged.

"Anything you want," he promised, his burning eyes singeing hers with their heat.

It was insane that he should want her so, but Bria always was a little crazy. And apparently, she had an inner floozy that she'd contemplate later. Much later. After he made her come a time or ten.

Lips, tongue, and teeth nibbled and tasted as he teased her into a frenzy of desire and need. By the time he pushed his big body between her legs, she really was panting. He'd kept his promise, just as she knew he would.

His cock, so thick and hard, filled her until she thought she would die from the pleasure. He went still, allowing her body to adjust to his welcomed invasion, nuzzling her lips with his. She felt his hardness, his heat, pressed along her whole body, and she loved it.

It was indescribably beautiful and efficacious. Then he moved, and Bria's heart thudded in her chest.

"Mine," he growled, lifting her legs so she could wrap them around his waist.

Her heels dug into his tight backside as he moved harder, faster, deeper. Trench was insatiable. Already lasting twice as long as any previous, easily forgotten lover ever had. Her body hummed with pleasure and her belly warmed as the first wave of her climax spread through her.

"Oh yes," she moaned, biting him on the neck in her passion.

She'd never felt the need to do that before, but something told her to, and again she went with her gut. The man above her went rigid, eyes aglow as he spoke through his clenched jaw.

"You're mine, say it," he demanded, and she did.

"Yours!"

"Tell me you want this, Bria."

"I want this. Want you," she moaned.

Trench reared up, eyes gold, taking her with him.

He plowed into her then, earnestly, heightening her pleasure. And when she couldn't take it anymore, he bit down on her shoulder and her whole entire world went white hot with unparalleled ecstasy at his touch.

Trench roared above her, then eyes still ablaze, he mashed his lips to hers and she tasted him, and something coppery on his mouth. It didn't discourage, if anything, it made it better. His cock swelled again, and he moved slowly this time. Rocking into her with care and imprecise movements.

It was beautiful. It was lusty. It was better than anything, and she loved every minute of it. Eventually, she fell asleep, and he must have carried them to a bedroom because she woke up on clean sheets with a warm body next to hers.

"Bria," Trench said, concern in his eyes.

That was when the pain started.

CHAPTER EIGHT

ISLAND STRIPE PRIDE

uck. Oh fuck. FUCK. What did he do?

Trench felt like he was being hit by a runaway train. Emotion after emotion slammed into him, like freight cars, and he was powerless to do anything but take it.

"Bria! Fuck, talk to me. Are you okay?" he asked.

He was worried out of his mind, but he did not dare touch her again. The first time he tried that, she'd screamed louder, and tears flooded from her eyes. Trench had never taken a mate before, but he'd allowed instinct to take over. Clearly, his tiger had fucked up.

Rooaarr!

The beast objected, but Trench ignored it. Fuck. His mate was in pain, and regardless of what his animal thought, it was his fault. Whatever he did, he would kick his ass later. Right then, he just needed to help her.

Bria had fallen onto the floor and refused to move. He already knew she would not let him touch her, and he didn't blame her. Apparently, it hurt like fuck.

The sounds of her moaning in pain were like knives to his heart. Shit. What could he do? She was sweat drenched and shivering, curled into fetal position on the cold, hard floor. He didn't know what went wrong, but there was someone who might. Once he got his head out of his ass, he ran to his cell phone and called his Neta.

The leader of the Island Stripe Pride did not sound very happy when Trench explained what had transpired, leaving out all the naughty bits, of course. Yes, he told him they'd been intimate and that he'd claimed her. That was all he needed to know.

"What the fuck did you do?" snarled the Neta of the Island Stripe Pride.

Trench didn't appreciate the tone. Especially not when his mate was writhing in agony on the floor. But he allowed it, he deserved the man's ire.

Holy shit.

She really was his mate now. He'd taken her, fucked her, and claimed her with his mating bite. He'd been so overcome by his own need, and his Tiger's insistence that she was his, Trench had allowed his primal instincts to take over. That was dangerous for a man like him.

It was probably wrong for him to be filled with joy, but he could not help it. She was his. And his joy was second to worry, but his beast was oddly okay with the whole situation, though he did not like her to be in so much pain.

Dean Romero continued to chuff and haw at the other end of the line until Violet, his mate, and the Nari of the Island Stripe Pride, took the phone. Luckily for Dean, Trench had no desire to take over as Neta or he might have challenged the guy over all his snarling about human females and endangering his mission.

Far as Trench was concerned, Bria was his only mission. She was everything to him. But seeing her in pain was pushing his beast closer to the edge. He needed to help her. Now.

"Trench? This is Violet, now talk to me, what is happening?" Violet Romero asked in that same tone of voice he heard her use with her cubs.

The woman had a spine of steel, far as he could

tell. But she was fair and kind, a good Nari and mate to the Pride's only leader. Trench had the utmost respect for both her and Dean. He was just agitated.

"She's in pain, Nari. Something, uh, happened."

"I see," she replied knowingly. "You gave her your mating mark?"

"Yes, Nari."

"Did you ask permission?"

"Uh, sort of," he cleared his throat.

"Well, this should be interesting," Violet muttered. "Okay, Trench, I believe she is going through the *Puspa*. I experienced it, and it is no picnic. Especially if she is fighting her change."

Then Violet laid out some rules for him to follow and he ended the call with a promise to follow up. Oh fuck. He looked down at where his mate was curled into fetal position and narrowed his eyes. Her skin was dotted with goosebumps and beads of sweat. Bria's hair was plastered to her forehead, and her eyes were bleary with fever.

"Hey now," Trench said, kneeling down beside her.

He did not dare to touch her, knowing even the slightest pressure on her sensitized skin would feel like she was being stabbed by a thousand sharp knives. The Puspa was a magical process that literally meant change. It was looked upon as a blessing by Tiger Shifters.

Only granted by the Fates to those special couples who were destined to be together. Beings whose hearts and souls were so perfectly aligned, one would only benefit from the gift of becoming a Shifter. The Puspa was a fairytale to most. He wouldn't have accepted it so readily had he not known about Dean and Violet having gone through it already.

Their love story was one for the books. At least it had a happy ending. As Trench watched Bria suffer, he wasn't quite as sure of his own. That did not matter just then. He had to help her through this, somehow.

"Bria, can you hear me?"

At her slight nod, he knew she was in there somewhere, trapped inside the agony. It tore at him inside, but his Tiger sent him the strength to continue when he would've cried out for forgiveness. The beast sensed what was near, and it couldn't wait.

"When I bit you, claimed you as my own, I started an ancient process I did not know was possible. It is called the *Puspa*. It means something is waking up inside of you, but you gotta let it in," he continued, gritting his teeth.

"You can give me hell later, I promise I'll take it. But you have to stop fighting the change, kitten. You need to let it happen. Let your Tiger in," he pleaded.

He stayed like that, by her side, whispering to her apologies, promises, and pleading one after the other. Trench meant every word. He was so happy to claim her, but he never meant to hurt her. It was his fault she was transforming, but he promised her change would get easier each time she did it. Bria was becoming part of his world now.

Yes, it was permanent, but she would never have to face it alone. He begged her to let in her animal. To accept the beast that was now part of her body, heart, and soul. Just as she was a part of him. Fuck, he loved her. And he told her. Begged her to believe him.

"Please, kitten. I love you. Stay strong for me. Let her in, my love, so you can live. I will do anything, anything at all, if you just live through this."

Eons later, or maybe an hour and fifteen minutes, she stopped shaking. Finally. Bria opened her eyes slowly and Trench gasped. Instead of the warm brown he loved, they were a bright yellow-gold.

She blinked again, slowly, as if seeing the world for the first time. He supposed she was. Her skin rippled, face sharpening into the more angular shape of a big Cat, and fur proceeded from her pores.

Slowly, so he could watch, her body began to shake and tremble, and the scent of ozone filled the air. Then, so suddenly he would have missed it if he'd even blinked, she shifted.

Bria Grotto chuffed, then snarled, loudly. She sneezed when she took a whiff of her paw, and he grinned. Then she turned her Tigress' eyes on him and hissed.

He would take her anger. As long as she lived. He could take anything then.

Her enormous feline head butted into him, hard. But all Trench could do was laugh and smile. He was so fucking happy she was okay.

And did he mention lovely? Her Tigress was beautiful. Her hide was a soft orange that blended more to tawny, and her stripes were more bronzed than black. Unique, gorgeous, both were applicable to her in either human or Cat form.

"You are so beautiful, kitten," Trench proclaimed.

She chuffed and hissed, clearly pissed off. And he didn't blame her, but he was just so happy he could not stop smiling. Her big ringed tail batted against his head until he got the message.

"Come on. Let's go for a run," he murmured, scratching behind her ears.

The female Tigress really seemed to like that if her purr was anything to go by. Trench was still undressed, so that part was easy. He opened the big side door and was shocked to see it was dark already.

His cabin was in a private section of woods, so he was not too concerned with trespassers. The necessary signs had been posted, warning hunters away. He was relatively certain they were safe.

"Ready?" he said, grinning over his shoulder.

His shift flowed over him, and his larger Tiger roared, calling his mate forward. The female hissed, vaulting over him and heading for the woods. He didn't mind a game of tag. In fact, he relished running after his mate.

Bria took to her new shape like a fish to water, or a cat to darkness, he supposed was a better analogy. He certainly enjoyed it when Stevie Nicks sang about that, anyway. Though Bria was way better than any rock song heroine.

His heart squeezed as he gave chase. For hours and hours they ran. All through the night, climbing trees and jumping in the creek. They fished, ate, and napped together under the stars. Bria taking to her fur better than he'd expected.

The sound of a twig snapping far too close caught his attention and Trench growled a warning. It was morning already. They had slept through the night in their fur. It had been wondrous and amazing, but now it was over. Time to face the new day in their human skin.

Grrr.

"Relax, it is just us," Dean Romero, his Neta, spoke before entering the clearing.

Trepidation ran through Trench. He knew what this meant. Throughout the night he'd picked up on thoughts and feelings from his mate, but her change was too new for them to be able to telecommunicate like some Shifter mates could. He had yet to speak with her.

And now that it was in his immediate future, Trench did not know what to say. Fuck.

Bria stood, alert and wary as Dean stepped into Trench's territory with Violet, the Pride Nari, by his side. His Tiger snapped at the intrusion, but the gentle swatting of Bria's tail against his side reminded him of what was really important.

Her. Always her. Only her.

Trench rubbed his head on the Tigress, pushing her gently behind him. Then he shifted to his human shape.

"Why are you here?" he questioned.

Dean stood silent, waiting. At the last minute, Trench remembered to avert his gaze lest he challenge the Neta, for fuck's sake. Violet snorted a laugh, then nodded at Bria, her smile calming and welcoming to the new Shifter.

"We are here to make sure you didn't do something we would have to clean up," Dean said, slightly annoyed but not angry.

That was good, at least. He knew he'd fucked up. But Trench had hoped to have time with Bria to talk to her before they had to return to normal life.

"The Shifter Council has a meeting set up for tomorrow. They want updates, Trench. We need your mate to come in," he said.

"No---"

The two men snarled and hissed, but stopped when Violet cleared her throat. Trench was no fool. He knew enough to heed a warning from a pissed off Tigress. She'd been kneeling by Bria, the two communicating without words as some Shifters were capable. Now, the Nari stood and faced both men.

"We are going back to the cabin so Bria can dress. You can follow and protect us or stay out here and measure your dicks. Your choice," she said.

Dean growled and moved to follow his mate, Bria

already ahead of them all. Trench took the rear. He tried not to listen to the Neta complaining to his wife about looking at another male's dick. Nudity was part and parcel of the whole Shifter thing, but it was funny to hear such a powerful man talk about it.

"How long will you need?" Dean asked Trench before he stepped inside.

"A few minutes, Neta."

"Okay. We parked beside Alex's car. He is going to kill you, by the way."

Trench nodded. What did he care? He mounted the stairs to the master bathroom. But Bria was already in there, he could hear the shower. He wanted to go inside with her, to join her under the warm spray, but he didn't dare presume.

So much had happened in so short a time. He grabbed some things and moved to the outdoor shower to wash and dress for the trip back home. When he was done, he was shocked to see Dean waiting for him. Alone.

"Where is Bria?"

"She wanted some time alone. Violet suggested they go back together. And I need to talk to you," Dean said, daring Trench to question him.

"Alone? How long have they been gone?"

"A few minutes. NO worries, Trench, they have an armed detail with them."

"But still," he began.

"Indeed. I understand. Let's go then," Dean said, cutting him off before he could voice his worry.

Shit.

His Tiger scratched against his skin, wanting him to haul ass. Now that he'd had a taste, he wondered if he could ever survive without her. With any luck, he would never have to find out.

"We need to talk," the Neta began, but Trench had one word in his head. And it was on instant replay.

Mate. Mate. MATE.

CHAPTER NINE

ISLAND STRIPE PRIDE

"I don't get it," Bria said.

She sat back against the plush leather seats in the rear of the luxury Lincoln Navigator with the Island Stripe Pride's own Nari, their term for female Alpha. She was trying to get used to the fact that her eyesight was like ten times better than ever, as was her hearing.

"It takes a moment," Violet said, a knowing smile on her face. "You know, to get used to it all. Being a Tigress. It's like the world is suddenly in high definition, right?"

"*Ohmygahd.* Yes, that is totally it!"

"Wait till you get hungry. And I don't know if steak or salmon was ever your thing, but you are going to start to crave it."

"Love steak, only like raw salmon or smoked."

"Then you better stock up. Smoked salmon is like chocolate for my beast. She loves it. And when I was pregnant, I couldn't get enough."

"You have kids?"

"*Cubs*. We call them cubs, and yeah, we have two," she grinned.

"Nice. Congrats."

"Thanks. Now let's get to the good stuff. Your mate will never cheat on you, and he will do everything he can to keep you safe and make you happy. Even if it means taking on the whole world," she explained.

"But how can I be sure of all that?"

"Sweetie, Shifters are not like regular guys. You see, taking a mate is more sacred and permanent than marriage. Both man and beast have chosen you, and on top of that, so have the Fates."

"The actual Fates? They are real?"

"Sure. Why not? You turn into a half ton Tigress, and you have a problem with believing in the Fates?"

"Good point," Bria murmured.

"I've known Trench a while now. He is a good man. A powerful Enforcer. Loyal and trustworthy---"

"Yes," Bria interrupted. "It's why I stayed with him. You see, I kind of get these feelings sometimes, like women's intuition. My grandmother had it. She called it her *knowing*."

"Wow. That is awesome," Violet said, sounding sincere.

"I guess it is, but anyway, I knew I could trust him."

"I see," Violet grinned. "Do you love him?"

"Yeah," Bria said softly. "I think I do. Am I crazy?"

"Oh, no honey, you aren't crazy," Violet scooted closer and put a friendly arm around Bria, allowing her to cry on her shoulder.

"I feel like an idiot. I am so sorry," Bria said, grabbing a tissue and blowing her nose.

She'd sneezed on the Nari, the most important female in the whole Pride. And not once. More like twenty times.

"Um, are you allergic to cats?" Violet asked.

"A little," Bria confessed.

"Well, maybe you can see an allergist? Anyway, did I mention sex with your mate is going to be fantastic?"

"It was so good---"

"Oh yeah, but just wait. It gets better," Violet said, wagging her eyebrows.

"Really?"

"Oh, yeah. Best. Sex. EVAH!"

The driver cleared his throat, and both females laughed. Bria was still kinda pissed at Trench. The sexy hunk of a man hadn't exactly explained what was going to happen after they'd boinked. But she wasn't mad. Not really. And Violet was right. It was the best sex ever.

"So, um, explain to me what happens now. I mean, like in my life."

"Well, Trench claimed you with his bite. It's like marriage, but a lot more permanent. Now what I am about to tell you might sound like you have no choice," Violet continued. "But that is far from the truth. Before I begin, Bria, I want you to understand that if you don't want to stay with him, I will do everything I can to help you."

Bria looked into the woman's eyes and nodded. Her woman's intuition alarm wasn't ringing, so she knew the female spoke the truth. The Nari seemed to accept her silence for acceptance, and she continued to explain just what had happened to her. After a few minutes of shared silence, Bria exhaled.

"It's a lot, huh?" Violet asked.

"Yeah. I do have some questions, you know being a vlogger and all," she began and rolled her eyes at her own silliness.

After all, she was a journalist of sorts. And the questions would not stop coming in the second she started voicing them. Bria was shocked and amazed to realize her own imagination was nothing compared to the wonder, the complicated glory, and the boring bureaucracy that made up the Shifter world.

"A Council? That sucks."

"It is a bit boring, but like with any civilization, it is necessary, isn't it? We have rules, Bria, and they are meant to keep us all safe. If people went around exposing us, well, what would happen?"

"Nothing good," Bria agreed.

"Can you explain more about the Puspa? Why is it legend? I mean, it happened to you *and* me."

"Actually, it is very rare, sometimes only happening once or twice in a single Pride. Fated mates are gifts from the universe, Bria," she said. "If Trench's bite preceded the Puspa, then I'd say you two were meant to be."

Meant to be? She pondered that over the long drive back to Manhattan. How could Bria be meant to be with a man she knew for only twenty-four hours? It was impossible. Wasn't it? Then again, Grandma Grotto loved telling the story about how she'd met and fell in love with Bria's grandfather the first time she set eyes on him.

"He walked into Church, and I was at the podium leading the offertory song when our eyes met. It was like lightning striking. He waited for me outside and we went to town for some ice cream, and I fell in love over mint chocolate chip."

Bria always loved that story. Her story was not as romantic, of course. She'd been trying to verify a video that proved Werewolves existed when she was attacked by a group of them, twice.

Then Trench showed up at the request of his boss, the Neta, under orders from the Shifter Council of New York City. His job was to do something to ensure she wouldn't let the cat out of the bag, no pun intended. After the encounter with the Wolves, she'd passed out, and he'd bought her to his cabin in upstate New York.

Within a matter of hours, they'd done more than she'd managed in some of her relationships that had lasted months. They had talked, eaten a meal together, and had the best sex of her life. Oh, yeah, and while they'd fucked, Bria had been bitten, and now she had a big furry alter ego.

"That about sums it up," she muttered.

"What was that?" Violet asked.

"Nothing," she replied.

"Look, I know this is difficult to process, but I assure you, you are safe. We would never hurt you. You are part of the Pride now. Besides, Trench would go on a rampage if a single hair on your head was harmed."

"What now?"

"Did I mention mated males were overly protective to the point of being homicidal maniacs?"

A snort from the front of the car earned the driver a glare from the Nari. She cleared her throat, and the man started whistling.

"Don't mind him. Carter Marrow, this is Bria Grotto," she made the introductions. "He's not our regular driver, which is why he doesn't know how to keep his fat mouth shut."

Violet was teasing, but the man whimpered as if heavily insulted. The whole thing made Bria laugh. Once that was out of the way, the three of them chatted about the Pride, and life for Tigers in the big city. Bria was interested to learn that the pride owned *ISP Inc.* and one of their holdings was a resort in the mountains.

An entire mountain getaway reserved for Shifters, but especially Tigers, sounded outstanding to her. Maybe when this whole thing with the Council was over, she and Trench could go for a weekend and get to know each other.

"What about my family?" she asked.

"Like your parents? Best to keep them out of the loop, for now," Violet replied.

"Okay. No worries. They're not big believers in the supernatural, despite my vlog," she muttered.

"Oh yeah, I've been streaming your show, and I think I have an idea for you."

Violet smiled. That launched an entirely new and lengthy discussion. Typically, Bria was not a fan of those types of conversations, but the Nari was bright, as she was fierce and friendly. Her ideas were solid, and Bria liked the sound of them a lot.

"We're here," Carter interrupted a short time later.

"Wow, that was fast," Bria murmured, gathering her notes.

"Time flies," Violet replied.

The car had stopped at an enormous building with the *ISP Inc.* logo chiseled into the cornerstone. Eyebrows raised, she looked at the high rise skeptically. Violet had explained that she was being brought to the building that housed most of the Island Stripe Pride within Manhattan. Most lived outside the city, but this was a safe space for them under the protection of the Neta and the Nari themselves.

"You don't have to go to his apartment," Violet said quietly as they rode in the elevator.

"No. It's alright," Bria said.

Actually, she was looking forward to a little time to explore Trench's space without an audience. Carter, the big bald Tiger male who'd driven them, walked her to Trench's space and unlocked the door. He'd kept his comments light and friendly, but did not look her in the eyes as he stepped back to allow her entry.

"Trench should be arriving within the hour, but I will be monitoring the hall here. Just yell if you need anything."

"You're going to wait in the hall?"

"You haven't even been mated for a full day, so I don't expect you to get it. Trust me on this, though. Trench is going to be highly agitated when he gets home from all the worry. I am just trying to do the guy a solid."

"Oh," she said. "Should I be afraid?"

"Of your mate? Why on earth would you be scared of him? Look, Trench is a good guy, and he would cut off his own tail before he would ever hurt you," Carter replied easily.

"Okay. One last question," she said, sick of looking at this guy's cheek or head.

"Why won't you look me in the face? With Violet, I mean with the *Nari*, I assumed you would not meet her eye because she's more dominant and has a position of power, but with me-" Bria let her voice trail off.

"Um, yes and no. But for you, I am averting my gaze out of respect for your newly mated status, Ms. Grotto. We are predatory Shifters," he further explained. "Maintaining prolonged eye contact is not only a way of announcing a physical challenge, but it is also a way of expressing desire. It would be highly disrespectful to Trench, and to you, if I were to covet his mate."

"Oh. Wow, that is a lot to remember."

"Look, just try to catch my gaze," he said.

Because she was interested in learning more, she went ahead and tried. Bria stood directly in front of the stupidly tall male. He had to be six and a half feet, not as big as Trench, but still large.

Sheesh. Was no one small here? Anyway, once she did that, she tried staring, then glaring at the man. But it was difficult. In fact, it made her Tigress snarl and hiss.

Even though she managed to do it, she had to

admit he was right. Meeting Carter's golden gaze was seriously uncomfortable after all of twenty seconds.

Wow, that was intense," she said, exhaling. "Lesson learned."

Bria smiled and laughed, tossing her hair behind her shoulder and Carter grinned and rubbed the back of his neck. Unfortunately, the agitated male who'd come upon them had no way of knowing that Bria was laughing and Carter smiling because he'd been proven right. But, before she could explain to Trench, Bria learned what Carter had been trying to teach her with a full on demonstration from an incensed mate.

Rrrrooarrrr!

"Wait!"

Bria tried to explain, but she was not foolish enough to get between two adult Shifter males. Especially once they'd swapped skin for fur. Big hands grabbed her by the arms, placing her behind the large frame of Dean Romero, the Pride Neta, while Trench and Carter proceeded to beat the shit out of each other.

"Why aren't you stopping this?" she asked angrily.

"I will. One second," Dean replied, obviously amused.

The Neta seemed to be enjoying the spectacle. Bria was so telling Violet. Ugh! She crossed her arms in annoyance.

Men. Can't live with 'em. Can't turn them into throw rugs. Grrr.

CHAPTER TEN

ISLAND STRIPE PRIDE

T rench exited the elevator in rare form. His skin itched, the Tiger in his mind's eye hissed and paced. He was angry. He was hungry. And he was horny. He wanted his fucking mate. Now.

Was he a raging, possessive asshole?

Yep.

And he would own that shit, too. Later. After he found his wayward little kitten.

Mine.

The whole ride home, Dean had been acting like a total fucking prick. He didn't even let him speed! Using his Alpha voice to ensure Trench had no choice but to listen, the fucker made him do the actual speed limit the entire way back to the city.

He could not wait to see her. *Bria*, his Tiger breathed her name. The beast was just as anxious as he. And it wasn't just the threat of those Wolf assholes that made him angry. It was the fact he missed her.

Shit. Trench was acting like a total fucking pussy.

Takes one to know one, his Tiger replied.

Apparently, everyone's a fucking comedian. Even Cats. SMH.

The second Trench stopped the car, he jumped out, slamming the door. She was close. Trench sniffed, picking up her scent in the air. Slightly faded, her vanilla citrus fragrance teased the beast within so much he was practically drooling in the elevator car all the way up to his floor.

There was so much to discuss. So much that he needed to tell her. The first and foremost being that he was sorry for rushing her, but he would never be sorry for claiming her. She was his whole heart, whether she believed him or not. And if not, then he vowed to work every day to earn her trust, and to be worthy of her as his mate. He had no choice. Trench was in love with her.

He swallowed hard, wishing the steel box would move faster, for fuck's sake. It was difficult to admit, but fuck yes, he did. He loved her.

But did he love her enough to let her go? That was something Dean had brought up, and his beast had gone a little crazy. In fact, he needed a new steering wheel cause he damn near crushed the thing when his Neta had posed the question.

"Shit," Dean muttered once the doors opened.

Mild curiosity had Trench looking up, and then everything turned red. Instead of finding his precious mate inside his apartment safe and warm, he saw that backstabbing motherfucker Carter eyeing his woman like she was a tasty piece of cake.

"Motherfuckerrrrrooooaaarrrr!" Trench roared, going a little bit berserk.

Like. Literally. Trench exploded into the hallway. His claws aiming for the two-faced SOB. No sooner had he landed a solid punch to the fucker's jaw, then the other man changed his skin for fur.

The hall was pretty cramped for two Tigers to tussle, but caution and common sense were both overthrown by Trench's fury. Thankfully, Dean had tucked Bria behind him, and on some other level, Trench knew he would not allow her to get hurt.

Incapable of stopping, he wrestled and clawed, bit, and shook the other, equal in size Tiger. He'd never felt such rage so fast or sudden. Yeah, he'd killed, but it was never personal. Not like this.

"ENOUGH!" roared Dean, but only when he said it again using his Alpha voice did Trench loosen his jaw, dropping the other Tiger to the carpeted floor.

Did he have the urge to bury him beneath the dirt? Yes. He just needed to find some dirt. Maybe he could drag him to the rooftop garden? Good idea.

Grrr.

"Carter, go see if the doc is available to clean you up. Trench, get your ass inside and talk to your mate before she clocks you over the head. Not that you don't deserve it. Bria, you okay?"

She nodded while Trench shifted back to human at the same time as Carter. The man had some wicked looking cuts and bruises, but judging from his own less than stellar feelings, he imagined he looked just as bad.

"I was just teaching her about being a Shifter man. She wanted to know why I wouldn't look her in the eye," Carter explained, averting his gaze from the still angry Enforcer.

"Fuck man, I---" Trench tried.

Bria stomped her feet, and walked inside, her posture angry as her expression. Okay. So, he was a total dick.

"Better go talk to her, man. I'll be fine," Carter replied.

"Just get going, you fuckheads," Dean muttered, leaving them to it.

"Congrats, man, and trust your instincts. She'll make you a good mate," Carter finished before limping away.

"If she'll still have me," Trench grumbled.

He was getting blood on the tile. Shit. He'd need to take a shower, but first he wanted to make sure she wouldn't bolt. Trench tracked her scent to the kitchen, where she had placed his previously unused kettle on the stovetop.

"Bria---"

Her head snapped up, and she turned to look at him. Her eyes were wide and gold, and he knew she was having trouble controlling her Tigress.

Dammit.

"Here," she growled, her voice thick with her animal.

She'd tossed him two towels and gestured to the sink. Trench stepped forward, washing the blood from his hands and his face. He wiped away the water, his wounds already healing. Neither man had really wanted to hurt the other. He realized that as he took in the shallow scratches and scrapes.

Bria inspected him, wiping spots he'd missed.

And not too gently. Fuck. But he would take it. He deserved it.

Trench was a selfish prick flying off the handle like that. Look at him, standing there, blood on his hands. Like a fucking caveman, when she was everything opposite. Everything sweet and soft and light and beautiful.

"Bri---"

But he didn't finish, cause she'd thrown herself into his arms. A sob wracked her body once, and Trench panicked. But then, she was kissing him.

Fuck, she was really kissing him.

Bria had launched herself at him and had her mouth fused to him, and her hand on his cock. He'd caught her, of course. Always would.

Cupping her ass, he kneaded the globes, holding her fully clothed body against his nude one. There was nothing better than the feel of her soft curves against the hardness of his own flesh and the taste of her mouth as she kissed him with everything she had inside.

Mine.

"Bri---" he knew he had things to say, but she wouldn't let him. Her small hands covered his mouth, and she was shaking her head fiercely.

"Nuh uh. You would have gotten a chance to talk if you hadn't done all that, but not now. No way."

"Bu---"

"Listen to me, Trench, I need you to just shut the fuck up and fuck me. Now. Like right now," she demanded.

Yesssss. Mine.

The Tiger inside him peeked through his eyes, he knew it when he saw hers looking right back at him.

The fight had turned his female on, and Trench was all about pleasing his woman. He knew they had to talk, but she was clawing at his shoulders and growling deep in her throat.

The sexy sound had his cock harder than a baseball bat. The metal kind. And damn, but he was dying to bury the thing to the hilt inside her tight heat.

He dropped her on the counter, tearing at her leggings and the little slip of silk she wore beneath it. Urgency rode him hard, but fuck, he was gonna have a taste of her first.

Her shirt was still on, but she never looked sexier, legs spread, head thrown back, mouth wide open. Trench was already on his knees, mouth closing over her sweet sex by the time she screamed his name.

Bria moaned aloud, rocking her hips in time with his tongue. Her fingers threaded in his hair, she pulled on it, pushing him harder against her mound. Fuck, but she was gloriously wanton. Sweeter than pie, and more savory than whiskey. He lapped at her slit, collecting all her juices and swallowing them down like they were precious to him. And they were.

Lick after lick, he swallowed her down, then she was coming, and by the gods, it was beautiful. Her brown eyes flashed gold as she tried to catch her breath. His sweet mate caressed his face while he slowed his ministrations. Trench never wanted to stop licking her, and from the way she bit her lower lip, he knew she wasn't inclined for him to stop, either. Not any time soon.

Still, the counter wasn't very comfortable. With his mouth still on her, Trench slid her forward, lifting her legs over his shoulders, he had his hands supporting her back when he lifted her. Bria let out a surprised gasp, but she laid back, trusting him to keep her aloft and pleasured with his tongue.

Her utter faith in him was humbling. Evidence that there was, in fact, a God, or gods somewhere in the ether. He dropped her gently on his enormous bed and fucked her with his tongue and fingers. When she came one more time, he slid up her body, relishing her release. Then he filled her with one hard plunge and rolled them over.

"Trench," she moaned.

Damn, he sure loved the sound of his name on her lips. Promised himself he'd get to hear it often. That was *if* he played his cards right. And he would. Just for that, he would do anything.

"Ride me, kitten."

Fingers gripping her luscious hips, Trench laid back and watched his mate as she moved. First, in slow, soft slides, up and down his dick. Then she grew confident, lost in the pleasure his body could bring her. Bria's head was tossed back as she began to move in earnest. Her sweet pussy squeezed and tightened, fuck it felt so good.

Like coming home. Like coming apart and back together again.

Fuck, he was going to come. Soon. But not without her. With his thumb, he found her clit, stroked the nubbin while she pumped faster and faster.

"Close. Gonna," she moaned.

Trench sat up, tugging one cotton covered nipple between his teeth. He grabbed her waist and alternated lifting and slamming her on his cock, over and over, harder and faster, until she shattered all over him. Her hoarse cry echoed in the room as she came, and just before he did, pain exploded on his shoulder, followed by the most profound pleasure of his entire existence.

His sexy kitten had claimed him with her bite.

"Fuck," he roared as her sex wrang out every bit of bliss he had to offer.

They collapsed together on the bed. His cock was still buried deep inside her as they both slipped into a dreamless sleep. They woke up hours later still entwined, only his dick was hard once more.

Trench held her close as he made love to her that time. Lips meshed together, he never stopped kissing her throughout that slow, thorough lovemaking. Not once. This time, when he claimed her, he asked her clearly first. His blood racing, near to bursting his veins wide open, when she said yes, again.

"I love you," Bria whispered.

She collapsed against him, utterly spent and happy, so very happy he felt it inside of him. That telepathic communication, her *knowing*, whatever miracle it was, he felt her inside of him, and he knew what love really was then. His heart swelled ten times its normal size.

She loved him, really loved him, and Trench had never felt better than right then. Which was why he was an even bigger piece of shit than he'd ever suspected.

Fuck.

How was he going to tell her she had no choice but to shut down her vlog? Even with her new status as both Shifter and mated to a Pride Enforcer, Bria's vlog was dangerously close to revealing the supernatural world.

It wasn't something he could protect her from. Not now. Maybe not ever. And the knowledge was driving him insane. There was only one thing for sure. Trench wouldn't survive without her. He wouldn't even want to try.

Mine.

CHAPTER ELEVEN

ISLAND STRIPE PRIDE

"That's ridiculous," Bria replied easily over a ridiculously decadent breakfast.

It was one of the perks of her new fast and furriest alter ego. Her metabolism was in super fabulous mode. Meaning, she could eat like a heifer and not get any fatter, *er*, fluffier. That was a nicer word. But anyway, her point was she would have to seriously work at it if she wanted to gain weight. Popping a still whistling sausage link in her mouth, Bria moaned. Real pork. Not grisly turkey.

Not that she hated turkey, she just didn't like ground turkey. It was weird and gritty. Chicken was better, but nothing could beat pork in her humble opinion. And since chicken sausage links were not the easiest to find, she would rather skip it than go turkey.

Sigh.

Only now she didn't have to.

Hooray!

"Are you listening to me?" Trench asked, eyebrows raised.

Damn. He looked so good sitting at the breakfast nook in a pair of teal cotton boxer briefs. All those rippling muscles, so nice and tanned, and that *just got out of bed* tousled look on his black-streaked reddish brown locks. Yum. Like seriously, *yum yum*.

"What?"

"Bria, I know it's fast, but since you said it, I am saying it to---"

"So, you are saying that I am better than you in every way cause I said it first?"

"What? No. I am saying I love you too," he growled, but couldn't contain his grin.

"Awesome. So, now that we both admit I am totally loveable, what was it you wanted?" she asked, then screeched as she pawed through his fridge.

"*Ohmygahd.* Is this bacon? Real porky, fatty, delicious, thick cut, hickory smoked, no nitrates, bacon?"

"Um. I don't know how to answer that. It says it on the package, Bri," he replied.

"I love you!" she shouted.

"Because of my bacon?"

"Yes. And your sausage."

She said and could have cried if it wasn't true. And ridiculous.

"Kitten? I have no idea what you are talking about, but if it makes you happy, I swear I will buy you truckloads of the stuff. Just let me protect you."

Ooh, points for him. Bria squinted at the man. Knowing now that he was not above bribery. She'd tried reasoning with him, but she would just have to keep her own secrets for now. Besides, it was too much fun taunting him with breakfast meats.

"Mmm, you know I think I like sausage better than bacon," she said, eyeing his package and licking her lips.

Trench's cheeks went pink. His breathing stuttered, and determined as he was to have this conversation, Bria knew she had him where she wanted him. Mainly with his boxer briefs, *the aforementioned teal ones* around his ankles.

"Fuck, kitten. I am trying to k-keep. Oh gods, to keep you saf---"

"Mmm, taste good," she moaned around his mushroomed head.

In the last few seconds, Bria had foregone bacon and pork sausage for the real thing. Sinking to her knees on the cool kitchen tile, she didn't even mind the sting as she licked her mate's impressive cock from root to tip. Taking him in her mouth, she swallowed him down as far as he could go, loving the rumble that came from deep inside his chest. Proof that she was doing something right.

"Bria, love, that feels so fucking good," he growled.

When he would have gently pulled her away, Bria growled back. She wasn't about to let go of her prize. If someone had asked her just a day ago, she would have said oral sex was not something she was very interested in. But with him, that all changed.

Bria moaned around his incredible girth, using her mouth, tongue, teeth, and her hands to give him pleasure. Most surprising of all was the echoing thrill she felt with every one of his groans and grunts.

Yes, she was turned on. She slid one hand between her legs, rubbing her sex as she sucked him down. It was erotic and sexy, and she never wanted it to end. But when he came, she swallowed. Only when she had consumed every drop did Bria sit back on her heels, grinning like the cat, *er*, Tiger that got the canary.

Or in this case, the cream.

"Yum," she said, looking up at Trench's face.

His eyes glowed with his beast, and he looked one part satisfied and one part hungry. She was hoping the latter was for her. And luckily, he didn't disappoint. Trench bent down and picked her up as if she weighed nothing at all. Kicking off his boxer briefs, he backed her up to the wall, using it to secure her while he kissed her mouth, her breasts, everywhere he could reach.

"So fucking sexy, kitten," he growled, his voice more beast than man.

Then he was inside her, and Bria couldn't think anymore. She could only feel. Not a bad thing since so much of her life, she'd been an overthinker. This was beyond normal thought. This was pure ecstasy, and only he could take her there.

Later, when they'd showered and eaten, Trench sat on the couch with Bria in his arms. She snuggled against his chest, just loving the feel of him so solid and warm beneath her. Again, this was out of her range of experience, but it felt so right. And she was so damn comfortable, she didn't want to move.

"It's fast for you, isn't it?" he asked.

She looked up then, saw the worry and concern on his face. But more than that, she saw the love he had for her right there. Amazingly, she returned his feelings, his intensity. Bria knew she would never feel this way about anyone else.

All the fairytales and Hollywood endings she'd thought she'd outgrown came at her like a hurricane. This was real. She was in love.

"A little," she replied. "But that's okay. Fast is better than never."

He kissed the top of her head, and they sat there together. She never imagined she could enjoy a comfortable silence with anyone, but there she was. Sitting on her mate's lap in the middle of his enormous living room. The couch was a deep brown color, and soft as velvet.

It was a gorgeous space, and she especially liked the large ceiling to floor windows. The sun was lower in the sky then, but its warmth filled the room and Bria didn't think she'd ever been happier.

"What are you thinking about?"

"Hmm," she replied, nuzzling into him.

Her inner Tigress chuffed and purred. The beast was taking some getting used to, but mainly, she felt as if it were an extension of herself. A little snort escaped her as she imagined telling her mom she could turn into an animal. Would her kids be able to as well.?

Crazy. Cool. Cats. That's us, she thought and snorted again.

"Bria?"

"Oh, nothing really. I'm thinking that this is crazy," she replied honestly. She couldn't give him anything less.

"Which part?" he asked, and she felt him grinning against the top of her head.

"The part where I turn into an eight hundred pound predator is pretty bizarre, but I was thinking more about the part where I found the love of my life in a complete stranger with eyes that burn and a heart of gold."

"You know, no one else in the world would say that about me, right?"

"That's ridiculous," she replied. "Your eyes are like a bonfire, especially when your kitty comes out."

"My kitty?" he scoffed with mock annoyance. "And no, I didn't mean that part. I meant the part about having a heart of gold," he whispered at the last, as if it embarrassed him.

Bria wasn't having any of that. Straddling his

waist, she clasped her hands behind his neck and looked him straight in the eyes.

"You listen to me, Trench Tora, I don't care what anyone else in this world says, and neither should you. You are the most important thing in my world right now, and *I* say you have a heart of gold."

"Then it must be true," he replied, squeezing her waist and mashing his mouth to hers.

Would this ever get old? She wondered as his tongue slid between her lips and he kissed her with such tenderness she could have wept. To think Bria used to doubt her friends when they talked about guys kissing them stupid. Turned out, she was wrong.

Thank fuck.

CHAPTER TWELVE

ISLAND STRIPE PRIDE

Trench was enjoying this quiet time with his mate when a knock interrupted them. Her head sprang up, and eyes gold with her Tigress blinked up at him.

"It's time," he murmured, rubbing his thumb down her cheek.

Bria nodded and rose off his lap. He hated the chill that hit him the second they weren't touching, but Trench needed to have his head on straight for this.

The Shifter Council of New York City had grown in power over the last year. The moniker no longer worked since they handled Shifter affairs in all the tri-state area. New York, New Jersey, and Connecticut now falling under their purview. But business was business, and their reputation was such that they were loath to change it.

Bria was quiet as they rode the elevator down to the waiting convoy of cars that would take the Island Strip Pride Neta, acting head of the SCNYC, his Nari, Trench, Bria, and some guards. Whenever you had groups of Shifters, especially those who would be enemies in the wild, it was wise to have numbers on your side.

The Wolves certainly would. As he mulled it over in his head, Trench could not shake the feeling that this entire thing was a setup. It made no sense, though. Bria was a normal, or had been before the *Puspa*. What did she have to do with a Wolf Pack from the big city?

"Are you alright?" she asked, her brown eyes so trusting and sweet.

No matter what happened, Trench swore then that he'd kill the whole fucking lot of them if they threatened her in any way.

"Yeah, I'm alright, kitten," he replied, squeezing her hand. "How about you? Nervous?"

"I mean, a bit. What are they going to ask me?"

"Not sure. They will want reassurances from you that you deleted the footage."

"But I did. You saw me," she said earnestly.

It had been a surprise, actually. Last night, after they'd made love over and over again, Trench had gone to the kitchen for a drink of water.

Worry was keeping him from sleeping. He could've taken it out of her hands, took her laptop that was even then charging on the counter, and he could have smashed the thing. But that wouldn't help. Plus, she'd be pissed.

He'd turned around the second he'd heard her join him. Silently, she smiled and, as if she knew exactly what he'd been thinking, Bria went to her computer. She motioned him over, started opening files and deleting them while he watched.

"I've taken screenshots of the email with the video, as well as proof that I've deleted it from my hard drive and clouds."

"Bria, I didn't ask---"

"I know, but I'm a Shifter now, too. It's my secret as well as yours and I would never let anything bad happen to you, Trench. Not if I could help it," she'd replied.

Fuck, if he didn't love her already, he would've fallen right then. His heart burned with emotion, and he lifted their joined hands and kissed her palm.

"Don't worry. I won't let anything happen to you," he whispered, echoing the same sentiment she'd pledged to him the night before.

Bria nodded her head, and he knew she believed

him. Proof again that gods existed. This sweet, trusting woman had shown more faith in Trench than anyone else ever had.

The ride over to the meeting place was relatively short. But only because they were not responsible for parking. Carter, the same Tiger whose ass he'd kicked the day before, nodded at him and exited the passenger seat.

He would act as a second guard for Bria, just as Trench had requested. The man scouted the area, using the slightest change of expression to relay it was safe to move from his standpoint.

"Shall we?" Bria asked.

She sucked in a fortifying breath, and Trench nodded. He didn't like it, but what choice did they have?

Dean and Violet Romero were already inside. Unlike the other meeting, this was not open to the general public. Only a few Shifter leaders were gathered, and their personal guards. Which is why Trench tensed when the entire McLeesh Pack walked in scant minutes later.

"Well, well," their Alpha sneered. "I see you've brought the traitorous human. Hand her over, and we will take care of her."

"McLeesh," Dean replied. "You've come with

quite the show of strength, but what for? This was to be a friendly meeting---"

"Friendly? This *human* has threatened our kind! She must be dealt with, but if you cats don't have the stomach, we Wolves certainly do!"

McLeesh spat the word human like it was dirty, and Trench's Tiger growled in warning. His Wolves stirred behind him, some partially shifting, others snarling and flexing their claws. Trench felt his fangs descend. He noted Carter moving to flank Bria on the other side, and he approved. His mate trembled a little, and he couldn't blame her.

There had to be almost forty Wolves against twelve Tigers. Enough for them to do some serious damage, but the Tigers outweighed the Wolves, some of them three to one. It would be an almost fair, if bloody, fight.

"McLeesh? We talked about this," Blake Nero, the Vampire representative, spoke. "First, we must hear out the female."

The Vampire gestured to a chair, but Bria did not move. Smart woman. He shook his head slightly, and Blake's eyes raised in surprise. Since Vamps were notoriously hard to kill, Trench knew he wasn't worried about the less than friendly energy in the atmosphere of the meeting room.

"I see things have changed. I shall remove myself from this meeting, as it is now an entirely Shifter matter," Blake announced, surprising McLeesh.

"What?! How can you say that?" McLeesh began, but the Vampire had moved so quickly, he was gone by the time the old Wolf was done speaking.

"Bloodsucking fool," McLeesh growled. "It is of no consequence, we are here now, and we are the ONLY ones that can protect our secret. Now, it is time for you to step down, Dean. My Pack demands the right to act in our best interests. Destroying this human and that video is our top priority!"

"Your Pack? You mean the entire pack you brought here? Unacceptable, McLeesh. In fact, this show of force is a threat to all here and as the acting Chief of the Council, I am in my rights to find you in contempt," Dean said, replying to the Wolf's aggression.

"Fuck this. Give us the girl," McLeesh's son and Beta stepped forward.

The Wolves were getting antsy, and they hadn't even discussed anything yet. Fuck. This wasn't a meeting about how to proceed to protect the Shifter secret. This was a plot to take over the Council. This was an act of war.

Grrr.

"You might want to step back, pup," Carter advised.

Trench was holding onto his Tiger by a thread. Every protective instinct he'd ever felt multiplied by a million. He needed to get her out of there now. The demands the Wolves were making were unthinkable. McLeesh was going to pay for this. Even if Trench had to hunt him down and gut him like the dog he was.

Of course, he had no desire to take over a Wolf Pack, but maybe after he killed him, he could send the rest of them elsewhere. Planning ahead wasn't exactly a strong suit, but now that he had a mate to protect, he would have to start.

Unaware that he'd been growling the entire time, Trench looked down, stopping that rumbling sound as soon as Bria placed her soft hand on his chest. She looked at him once, her brown eyes clear and determined. He saw only a hint of her Tigress, which meant she was lurking there, ready to protect her human half, but only when called.

Good. That was good. After all, he was there, and Trench would not let one hair on her head come to any harm as long as he drew breath. That was a motherfucking promise.

"If I can address the Council and the Wolf Pack?"

Bria asked, surprising McLeesh and Dean into silence.

The two had been arguing hotly. But when the tiny female stepped forward, uncowering in front of both dominant males, Trench thought with more than a hint of pride in his mate, they stilled.

"Please," Dean invited, cordially.

"Mr. McLeesh, my name is Bria Grotto---"

"Your name is of no consequence. You are a normal, and you have no--"

McLeesh stopped when Bria, to Trench's horror, moved closer to the Alpha male. The man leaned forward.

Sniff. Gasp. Sniff sniff.

"Sh-she's been mated! You had one of your tom cats mate her," McLeesh snarled, accusing Dean.

"If you would stop your snarling," Bria tried. "I can explain."

"It does not matter. Even a mate who violates our trust---"

"QUIET!" Violet stepped forward and yelled, hands on her hips. "Geez. Let the woman speak!"

Dean's eyes twinkled, and he winked at his typically quiet mate. The female winked back, gesturing for Bria to continue.

"I have been running my vlog for a long time searching for proof of the supernatural," Bria began.

She addressed not just the Wolves and Tigers, but the Dragons, the Cougars, the Druid Priestess, and other representatives who'd just arrived to witness this meeting at Dean's invitation. Trench had known about it, but he was unprepared for the level of angst his Tiger would experience. All he wanted was to scoop his mate up and take her home.

Keep her safe and warm- and mostly naked, forever, in his den. Yeah. Good plan.

He rolled his eyes at his Tiger's thought process. Typical besotted male. Good thing his human half knew better. And he stood beside her, ready to pounce on any threat, while she spoke so eloquently about what she did.

"I never considered the consequences of my search, and for that I must apologize. But this video of the Wolf shifting was sent to me anonymously. Now, I've brought my laptop to give to the Council's tech experts, but I already deleted the footage from my hard drive and my clouds---"

"Are we to take the word of a human?" McLeesh bellowed, but Bria just rolled her eyes.

"McLeesh," Dean snarled in warning.

"And you, ha, we should trust you? What kind of

leader forces one of his own to mate with a normal?" the Wolf Alpha continued, trying to persuade the crowd.

"Maybe you need an allergy pill or something, Mr. McLeesh, because I am no longer human," Bria said, shifting only her eyes and staring at the suddenly pale Wolf.

"True, I have found my mate among the Island Stripe pride, but we weren't ordered to get together. It was fate, as I believe some of you might already know. As a result, I'm a Shifter now too, and your secret is now mine," she said, smiling now in the face of all those predators.

Fucking hell.

The woman was astounding, and Trench couldn't help but admire her bravery. She continued to explain about her new status and her vows to keep the paranormal world under wraps.

"This is all well and good, but what about her vlog? Is she going to continue to skirt our laws and hide behind her mate's tail?" McLeesh tried a new tactic.

Shit.

This was something Trench had already anticipated. He would never ask her to give up her work, but it was going to be tricky. Still, he'd leave New

York, the Pride, all of it, so she could keep doing what made her happy. Crazy how that was the most important thing to him, after her safety, of course.

"Actually," Bria said, surprising even him. "My vlog is temporarily undergoing reconstruction. You see, I will never stop being interested in the supernatural. I mean, now more than ever," she said and snorted adorably. "Being a Tiger has only made me more curious, but my new vlog is called *Once Written: Interviews with Paranormal Fiction Authors*. I already have my first guest booked," Bria announced, nodding at Violet Romero, who was a well-known paranormal romance author.

"Well, that is something," Noemi Donato, the Druidess representative, replied with a warm smile.

"Thanks," his sassy, brilliant mate replied.

"Will you be happy with that?" Trench asked, uncaring about anything else.

"Are you kidding? I've read everything the Nari has written under her pen name, *V.R. Stripes*. She is brilliant!"

He wanted to kiss her. But of course, some *soon to be dead* asshole interrupted.

Grrr.

"Wait. Wait! This is no guarantee that whoever sent the video won't try again. She has contacts. We must interview her to get their names," McLeesh spat and stuttered, clearly losing his grip.

The Wolves started shifting around and Trench's eyes narrowed. Something smelled funky. And it wasn't just the scent of dog in the room.

"I don't think that will be a problem," Bria said, nodding at Violet.

Just then, the Pride's Nari lifted her finger, and Carter, who'd been standing on the other side of Bria, nodded. He placed two fingers in his mouth and whistled. A moment later, a she-Wolf was brought into the room by one of their Tigers.

"Nancy?"

Bria growled, and he could tell his mate was pissed.

"Everyone, this is one of my former roommates. Her name is Nancy McLeesh."

The room erupted in outrage. Everyone tossing accusations and name calling, but the Nari whistled loudly, bringing everyone to attention.

"OMG! You people need to act like adults, and let her finish," she growled.

"Thank you, Nari," Bria said, smiling at the powerful female. "As you can guess, she's related to Alpha McLeesh, his niece, in fact. She sent the tape under his orders."

"Why?" one of the representatives asked.

"Well, she was always a bit of a *bitch*, but I had no idea until this morning how true that was. Wolf female and all," she added, with an extra pinch of sass.

"Nancy," Violet stepped in. "Tell everyone here what you did."

"I was only following orders---" the she-Wolf began, clearly frightened. "My uncle made me do it! He found out my roommate was a vlogger and researched her. He was just mad the Council chose a Cat over a Wolf to lead them---"

The McLeesh Pack started growling and chatting nervously. Some had already fled, others were starting to confess. The girl was sobbing, but the Alpha didn't seem to care for his niece. He lunged forward, and whether it was to get at Bria or Nancy, Trench could not be sure, and he did not give a fuck, either.

What kind of lowlife attacked females? Within a blink of an eye, Trench had the old dog by the throat. His claws unleashed, Trench snarled. Enforcer that he was, his beast demanded justice, but the newly mated Tiger in him also wanted blood. He looked at Bria and saw what she needed from him.

Keeping hold of his bloodlust, Trench flipped the

Wolf over and locked him down before the prick could do any more damage.

Then Trench roared his outrage, and the whole room stilled.

"Good job, Trench," Dean said, approaching with the Council's own security team.

They cuffed and tied the Werewolf up, using magically enhanced silver handcuffs and chains. He started to protest, so the guards added a muzzle. It was a good look on the traitor.

"Lock him up and gather the rest of them into a detention cell. Then call Rafe Maccon. We will ask the esteemed candidate for the next High Alpha of Wolves to determine what happens to the McLeesh Pack going forward."

Everyone agreed, but Trench didn't give a fuck about Wolf politics. He just wanted to get his mate back home.

Bria was safe and sound, and his. So very his. Nothing else was as important to him as that.

Mine.

EPILOGUE

ISLAND STRIPE PRIDE

"So let me get this straight," Trench began.

But Bria was only half paying attention. She was kind of lost in the way the moonlight was shining on those crazy colors she loved so much in his hair. They were both sitting up in the mess of sheets and blankets that littered their bed, feeding each other ice cream and kissing between bites.

It was her new favorite pastime. Kissing Trench, that was.

"You and the Nari discussed all of this on the ride back from the cabin, and you didn't even tell me?"

"Um, yeah, I guess," she said, taking the last bite of blackberry fudge swirl.

She placed the empty carton on the table and

crawled towards her mate, loving the way his eyes heated even when he was annoyed. Bria straddled his lap, and his arms came around her.

"Bria, why didn't you tell me? Didn't you trust me?"

"What?" she said, stopping mid kiss. "Of course, I trusted you. I told you that the first time I saw you."

"You did," he murmured, nuzzling her nose. "I remember."

"I was just caught up in you and this, and my Tiger, and I suppose it slipped my mind."

"Slipped your mind?" he asked, clearly not buying it.

"Maybe I wanted to surprise you," she replied, revealing a hint more of truth.

"I see," he growled.

Bria grinned and pulled the sheet off his lap, sliding her slick sex along his hardening cock. His nostrils flared, and she leaned, kissing him and marveling at the freedom she had to do so.

"Love you," he growled, holding her by the hips and lifting her.

"I love you, Trench," she moaned.

Trench lowered her slowly. Her pussy stretched as she took him deep inside her core. He filled her so damn good. And not just her sex, but her mind, her heart, everywhere.

Bria rocked her hips slowly, wanting to feel every inch of him. But it wasn't enough. Never would be. They started to move in earnest, panting and kissing, nibbling each other. Then he lifted her up, turned her over on all fours, and her inner Tigress growled in anticipation.

"Want you mate," he growled, more animal than man.

"Go on then, Trench," she said. "Come and claim what's already yours."

And he did. Even better, she claimed him right back.

Roarrr!

he end.

I really hope you enjoyed this Island Strip Pride book.
Do you want to learn more?

You can read all about Dean and Violet in The Tiger King's

Christmas Bride. And find out how the Pride Beta snagged his female in Claiming His Virgin Mate.

& Don't forget to look for the next book in this series, Tiger Denied.

Thanks for reading!
Del mare alla stella,
C.D. Gorri

HAVE YOU MET MY BEARS?

Looking for a Paranormal Romance series that is loads of growly fun?

Meet the Barvale Clan first in the Bear Claw Tales! A complete shifter romance series about 4 brothers who discover and need to win their fated mates!

Followed by two more spin off series, the Barvale Clan Tales and the Barvale Holiday Tales!

No cliffhangers. Steamy PNR fun. Go and read your next happily ever after today!

BEWARE... HERE BE DRAGONS!

The Falk Clan Tales began as my stories surrounding four dragon Brothers and how they find their one true mates, but when a long lost brother arrives on the scene, followed by a few more Shifters...what can I say? The more the merrier!

Each Dragon's chest is marked with his rose, the magical link to his heart and his magic. They each have a matching gemstone to go with it.

She's given up on love, but he's just begun.

In *The Dragon's Valentine* we meet the eldest Falk brother, Callius. He is on a mission to find a Castle and his one true mate, one he can trust with his diamond rose....

His heart is frozen; can she change his mind about love?

In *The Dragon's Christmas Gift* our attention shifts to Alexsander, the youngest brother of the four. He has resigned himself to a life alone, until he meets *her*.

Some wounds run deep, can a Dragon's heart be unbroken?

The Dragon's Heart is the story of Edric Falk who has vowed never to love again, but that changes when he meets his feisty mate, Joselyn Curacao.

She just wants a little fun, he's looking for a lifetime.

We finally meet Nikolai Falk and his sexy Shifter mate in *The Dragon's Secret*.

*Now available in a boxed set.

Look for The Dragon's Treasure in 2022!

Paranormal Romance Books:

Macconwood Pack Novel Series:

Charley's Christmas Wolf: A Macconwood Pack Novel 1

Cat's Howl: A Macconwood Pack Novel 2

Code Wolf: A Macconwood Pack Novel 3

The Witch and The Werewolf: A Macconwood Pack Novel 4

To Claim a Wolf: A Macconwood Pack Novel 5

Conall's Mate: A Macconwood Pack Novel 6

Her Solstice Wolf: A Macconwood Pack Novel 7

Also available in 2 boxed sets:

The Macconwood Pack Volume 1

The Macconwood Pack Volume 2

Macconwood Pack Tales Series:

Wolf Bride: The Story of Ailis and Eoghan A Macconwood Pack Tale 1

Summer Bite: A Macconwood Pack Tale 2

His Winter Mate: A Macconwood Pack Tale 3

Snow Angel: A Macconwood Pack Tale 4

Charley's Baby Surprise: A Macconwood Pack Tale 5

Home for the Howlidays: A Macconwood Pack Tale 6

A Silver Wedding: A Macconwood Pack Tale 7

Mine Furever: A Macconwood Pack Tale 8

A Furry Little Christmas: A Macconwood Pack Tale 9

Also available in two boxed sets:

The Macconwood Pack Tales Volume 1

Shifters Furever: The Macconwood Pack Tales Volume 2

The Falk Clan Tales:

The Dragon's Valentine: A Falk Clan Novel 1

The Dragon's Christmas Gift: A Falk Clan Novel 2

The Dragon's Heart: A Falk Clan Novel 3

The Dragon's Secret: A Falk Clan Novel 4

The Dragon's Treasure: A Falk Clan Novel 5

Dragon Mates: The Falk Clan Complete Series Boxed Set Books 1-4

The Bear Claw Tales:

Bearly Breathing: A Bear Claw Tale 1

Bearly There: A Bear Claw Tale 2

Bearly Tamed: A Bear Claw Tale 3

Bearly Mated: A Bear Claw Tale 4

Also available in a boxed set:

The Complete Bear Claw Tales (Books 1-4)

The Barvale Clan Tales:

Polar Opposites: The Barvale Clan Tales 1

Polar Outbreak: The Barvale Clan Tales 2

*Now in a boxed set and in audio!

<u>The Maverick Pride Tales:</u>

Purrfectly Mated: Paranormal Dating Agency: A Maverick Pride Tale 1

Purrfectly Kissed: Paranormal Dating Agency: A Maverick Pride Tale 2

Purrfectly Trapped: Paranormal Dating Agency: A Maverick Pride Tale 3

Purrfectly Caught: Paranormal Dating Agency: A Maverick Pride Tale 4

Purrfectly Naughty: Paranormal Dating Agency: A Maverick Pride Tale 5

Purrfectly Bound: Paranormal Dating Agency: A Maverick Pride Tale 6

Also available in 2 boxed sets:

The Maverick Pride Volume 1

The Maverick Pride Volume 2

<u>Dire Wolf Mates:</u>

Shake That Sass: Sassy Ever After: Dire Wolf Mates Book 1

Breaking Sass: Sassy Ever After: Dire Wolf Mates 2

Pinch of Sass: Sassy Ever After: Dire Wolf Mates 3

Also available in a boxed set:

Dire Wolf Mates Volume 1

Wyvern Protection Unit:

Trusting Her Protector

Tempting Her Protector

Tricking Her Protector

Standalones:

The Enforcer

Blood Song: A Sanguinem Council Book

EveL Worlds:

Chinchilla and the Devil: A FUCN'A BookSammi and the
Jersey Bull: A FUCN'A Book

The Guardians of Chaos:

Wolf Shield: Guardians of Chaos Book1

Dragon Shield: Guardians of Chaos Book 2

Stallion Shield: Guardians of Chaos Book 3

Panther Shield: Guardians of Chaos 4

Howl's Romance

Mated to the Werewolf Next Door: A Howl's Romance

The Tiger King's Christmas Bride

Claiming His Virgin Mate: Howls Romance

Twice Mated Tales

Doubly Claimed

Doubly Bound

Doubly Tied

Hearts of Stone Series

Shifter Mountain: Hearts of Stone 1

Shifter City: Hearts of Stone 2

Accidentally Undead Series

Fangs For Nothin'

Moongate Island Tales

Moongate Island Mate

Mated in Hope Falls

Mated by Moonlight

Shifters Unleashed Boxed Sets

Check out these amazing anthologies where you can find some of my books

and the works of other awesome authors!

Coming Soon:

Ash: Speed Dating with the Denizens of Hell

Hungry Like Her Wolf: Magic and Mayhem Universe

Shifter Village: Hearts of Stone 3

Midnight Magic Anthology (Water Witch)

Mouse and the Ball: A FUCN'A Book

Tiger Claimed

For Fangs Sake

EXCERPT FROM WOLF SHIELD: GUARDIANS OF CHAOS BY C.D. GORRI

What a day! Fergie McAndrews headed towards the pick-up truck she'd borrowed from her roommate for work that morning.

Of course, the thirty-thousand dollar certified used luxury car she'd splurged on earlier in the year was in the shop. Again.

Just another in a long line of bad decisions. After leaving a perfectly good job for a startup company, she was laid off three weeks ago and had to borrow money from her parents to pay rent. Wasn't that humiliating?

"This is the last time, Ferg," her step-monster had said *after she'd Venmo'd the money to her.*

God forbid the mechanic call and tell her the car

was ready. She wouldn't be able to pick it up for another week. That was when she got her first paycheck from her newest gig at L-Corp. Not a startup, but an older company with new offices in Bayonne, which was only a half-hour commute.

But to commute, you needed a car. Fergie had no choice but to borrow the old pick-up from her best friend and roommate, Jessenia Banks. It wasn't like she needed the truck. She worked from home these days. Besides, Fergie promised to fill it up and have it washed.

She huffed out a breath. It'd been a really long day. A crappy one too. Fergie wanted to love her new job. Really, she did. But so far, it was the pits. If Fergie wanted to be a librarian, she would've been one.

Research was her jam. Well, when it was interesting. She had a knack for sniffing out information and compiling easy-to-read spreadsheets and timelines. It wasn't the hard work that annoyed her. Her complaint was the content. The actual stuff her new boss had her looking up. It was beyond boring.

Why an enormous conglomerate like L-Corp needed old land surveys, cross-referenced with newspaper reports on accidents, crimes, etcetera. She had no idea. She'd been at it for weeks now. So far, she'd researched six locations given via GPS coordinates across Hudson County. Her new boss wanted everything, every little insignificant piece of information she could dig up.

That was the easy part. It was the hassle of the actual job that really made her want to give up. Every day she had to drive to Bayonne to pick up her work laptop she'd dropped off the night before with all of that day's findings. Every single night they wiped her computer clean.

Like she was going to run away with the secrets of what happened on 2nd and Washington sixty-years ago. Can you say paranoid? Ugh.

Fergie had always looked forward to working for a huge global company. It was supposed to be her ticket out of the Garden State. Traveling the globe, seeing new things, visiting far-off places was always a secret dream of hers. Well, that, and having her own walk-in closet full of gorgeous designer shoes.

Best secret dream evah! In her opinion, anyway. What woman didn't love shoes? Fergie hummed as she daydreamed about rows and rows of Blahnik's, Jimmy Choo's, Garavani's, Ferragamo's, and her personal favorites, Louboutin's on every shelf!

Don't judge. Fergie wasn't shallow, she just liked pretty things. Haters gonna hate. But every time she ran across a thrift or second-chance store, she'd search high and low to see what they had. That was how she'd scored the pumps on her feet.

They made her feel good about herself. Being five-foot two-inches short with more curves than a racetrack, Fergie had had more than her fair share of self-esteem issues growing up. Alright, so she was chubby. She could admit that proudly now.

If everyone looked the same, the world would be one boring as hell place. Fergie liked herself perfectly fine these days, in spite of all the times her step-monster tried to make her diet growing up. So she liked food and shoes. Big deal.

She worked hard to feed and clothe herself, so as far as she was concerned, no one had a right to comment. So what if she wanted some excitement in her life? Fergie was aware she was better off than most, but what was wrong with having goals?

She'd spent a lot of time thinking about how a woman like her could have an adventure. Travelling was the only thing she could think of. Of course, she'd been hoping this job would be the answer to that. Even travelling for work was better than being stuck.

Sigh.

So far, her plans had fallen flat, but hey, at least she was earning a paycheck. Her new boss, Mr. Offner, might be a strange man, but he signed her checks, and that was enough for now. Fergie had never seen more than a glimpse of him. All of her instructions usually came via email.

Most of the time she was able to compile her research quickly, then she'd head back to the office to organize it into neat little spreadsheets, and finally, she'd hand it all in with her laptop. But not today.

Mr. Offner sent her an email detailing everything she could dig up on one of the oldest places on record in the county. Of course, land surveys that old, along with police reports, newspaper articles, deeds, and sales records were nowhere she could easily access them.

After wasting hours at both the court house and municipal building, Fergie had been directed to the *second* public library. Apparently anything over a hundred years old was filed away in the godforsaken place. She'd been shocked to find an entire room filled with musty old archives. And wouldn't you know it, there was no cell service and no internet access. Plus, their phone lines were down. She'd had to photograph each page using her cell. When she got home later, she would send those photos like a fax to her boss along with her spreadsheet. If she could manage that before collapsing into bed.

EXCERPT FROM BOUND BY AIR BY C.D. GORRI

Troy Waman looked down at his smartphone to the little red arrow blinking on his map app, indicating he had reached his destination. He frowned pensively before shaking his head.

"What a fucking shithole," he murmured to himself as he exited the nondescript black SUV his Station Master, Rex, had given him for the job.

"Try not to scratch it," the tough Bear shifter had said with a barely contained growl after their meeting the day before last. After a thousand years of waiting, The *Wardens of Terra* were being called to duty and this was Troy's first assignment.

It took him a day and a half to make his way to Shadowland, New York from the little suburb in Virginia Beach where his Station was located. There were dozens of them across the continental United States and even more overseas, though he'd rarely been out of the county himself.

Troy rolled his shoulders and exhaled. He was the first from his Station to be called to duty. A fact that left him both proud and humbled at the same time. He'd trained damn hard since he was a child waiting for such an opportunity. Now he had it, and it was almost too much to bear.

Fuck and damn. It's time Troy, get your ass in gear. That was all the sympathy he had for himself. Why the hell should he have any at all? Troy Waman was no tenderfoot normal. He was a Warden of Terra. He didn't need to remind himself of the honor and duty that went along with his position.

The *Wardens of Terra* were an ancient group of elite warriors. All of them Shifters. Identified in their youth and trained throughout their preternaturally long lives, they were guardians as well as fighters. *Station Masters* led teams of Wardens across the planet.

Though they'd been deactivated sometime in the last millennium, Wardens were born, chosen, and trained every day with the distinct knowledge that someday, they'd be called upon to defend the earth. That day was here.

Troy Waman had been trained as a Warden since before he learned how to spell the word. His heritage was a mix of Anglo and Native American. His father's blood was a mix of tribes including Algonquin, Lenape, Cherokee, and a few others. He hadn't stuck around long enough for anyone to learn the rest.

He supposed he could get a DNA test, but that might raise too many questions with the normals. Especially in this day of advanced technology in biogenetics.

Besides, it was quite common in today's world to find Native American peoples descended from multiple tribes. Troy Waman was uncommon for an entirely different reason. He was a Shifter, a special race of dual natured beings with one foot in the supernatural world and one in the human. Troy was a *Thunderbird Shifter* to be exact. Something unique even amongst Shifters.

He stretched his long, lithe body as he stepped away from the vehicle. It was already dark out despite it being fairly early in the evening. *Daylight savings my ass.* He sniffed the frigid air. The unusually high winds made the cold seem even more bitter. The street lamp stuttered on the corner, a rusty fence squeaked, and a black cat crossed the street, ducking under some parked cars. Troy's frown deepened.

It looked like the setting of a B-horror flick. All it needed was some half naked co-ed to run down the street with a masked bogeyman stalking behind her, traditional blood-coated knife in hand. *Oh yeah.* They might call it *Shadowland Nightmare* or something equally cheesy.

He stopped his musings and used his heightened senses to take in the downtrodden area around him. It would seem upstate New York wasn't all orchards and sprawling suburbs. He smirked as the "I love New York" song ran through his head. *Yeah, right.*

Apparently, parts of the Empire State were as fucked up as the street where he was born in Newark, New Jersey. He'd visited that shithole back when he was in his teens just out of curiosity. What a mistake that had been! He'd left almost as soon as he'd arrived. His extended family had been, shall we say, less than welcoming.

His gray-haired grandmother had screamed and crossed herself when he stepped over her threshold. He was what they called a *skin walker*. They feared and loathed him as something evil. Him evil? Like he was the motherfucker who knocked-up some unsuspecting normal and left her ass with a Shifter baby.

He was not evil, but he was something they did not understand. He'd been angry and ashamed that day. He'd crashed through his grandmother's kitchen to hitch a ride back down to his Station in Virginia Beach.

In his youth it was more like a military training camp, but it was all he knew of home. After all, it was where he'd lived his entire life. He'd made his peace and settled fully into his life there.

The incident with his grandmother had happened over a decade ago, when Troy had stolen his records out of Rex's office. Still, the memory remained fresh in his mind as if it were only yesterday. The fucked-up street where he was standing only brought back the painful reminder that he'd come from the same kind of squalor. *Fuck this*, he thought.

The pungent scent of despair washed over him. *Reminding him*. A young man with a hood pulled up over his head, eyed him from the street corner. *Drug dealer. Shadowland* indeed. It was an apt name for this shamble of a neighborhood.

The young man continued to stare until Troy allowed his beast to shine through. His golden eyes pinned the errant youth through the inky darkness of the night. Startled, the kid dropped the bag he was holding and ran down the alley.

Punk. Troy walked over and picked up what he had so hastily left behind. A couple of grams of crack cocaine and heroin, *probably cut with Fentanyl.* There were also various sized baggies full of what smelled like some below average marijuana and half-rotted psychedelic mushrooms.

Just your garden variety of illegal substances to be found on most street corners in neighborhoods like this one. *Fucking normals.* He frowned and dumped the still sealed contents down the closest storm drain. He sent a quick text to Rex earmarking the location.

Rex would make sure the local police department got an anonymous tip to retrieve the narcotics before someone got hurt. Recreational drug use, mainly the opioid epidemic, was wreaking havoc amongst the humans with more and more of them succumbing to their addictions.

It was troubling, but not Troy's problem. Shifters were extraordinarily hard to kill. Most human drugs had little to no effect on supernatural beings. *Normals,* he growled the thought, *such weak creatures.*

To be fair, Shifters had vices too. He just had little experience with it. Cecil, a Station-mate of his, had an adrenaline addiction. He was always putting himself in dangerous situations, even during simple training exercises. Fernandez, a Jaguar Shifter, was always trying to get into some chick's pants. *Sex addict*. And he knew of others who channeled their energies into ways he considered to be mostly unproductive.

His opinion, for sure. He'd always been something of a loner by nature. There weren't many Thunderbird Shifters around. Hell, he was the only fucking one he knew of in this part of the world.

He didn't blame or judge his Station-mates for their proclivities. Most of the Shifters he knew had large appetites which included food, exercise, and sex.

Troy had certainly explored that part of him. He wasn't a man-whore or anything, but he'd had his share of women. None of them mattered to him. Just a means to satisfy the occasional itch.

Troy was determined to live his life as a Warden of Terra alone. He never expected to find anyone willing to share what was a potentially deadly existence.

Those who followed the Darkness and evil were always looking for ways to gain the upper hand and it was his job to stop them. The way he saw it, it was an honor and a duty to serve.

He shared this great responsibility with the entire

organization. The core belief of the Wardens was based on one indisputable fact Shifters had walked the earth since the dawn of time, even before humankind; therefore, they were responsible for the well-being of the entire planet and all its inhabitants. Especially those who were inherently weaker. Mainly females and *normals*.

There were other supernaturals who believed humans, or normals as they referred to them, were a blight on the planet. Those creatures wished to destroy them and take over.

Demons, Dark Witches, and a whole plethora of evil beings sought the destruction of the normals and the world they lived in. *Idiots! Did they even realize if they destroyed the world, there would be nothing left? Where the fuck would they live?*

Of course, the supernatural world had many agencies that worked towards the common goal of saving the planet. The *Order of the Guardians,* for example, were responsible for policing the various factions of supernaturals.

Shifters generally tended to ally themselves with the Guardians. Sure, there were *bad* Shifters, but he'd never come across any willing to follow the Dark. Simply because most agreed the destruction of the world could not be allowed to happen.

Different Packs and Clans, etcetera, of course, had different ideas. Some wanted to remain secret, others wished to come out, and other still wanted to rule the weaker humans. It was a whole fucking thing, and they argued about regularly.

Troy didn't know from any of that. He spent little time in the human world. His efforts better spent making himself worthy of being a Warden. Training, exercise, and following orders. That's what Troy lived for, it was why he was chosen.

Thunderbird Shifters were very rare. *Special.* He scoffed at the stray thought. But no matter what way he looked at it, Troy was indeed unique. In more ways than one. He was born *marked* by the stars. A *Shifter of Terra.*

From infancy, he was told he carried the power of his sign within him. *Aquarius* ruled his destiny and it would aid him in the never-ending battle against the forces of darkness.

Every single Warden he knew was a Shifter like him. They were the fiercest warriors on the planet. Like many others throughout the last thousand years, Troy, *a Shifter child who was marked,* was taken from his parents and trained by his Station Master until the time when he would be called into use.

All that time, he thought, *and here I am.* He tried to

ignore the pressure building inside of him. He felt anxious. His animal pressed against his psyche, comforting him with his presence.

The significance of the moment was not lost on him. The Wardens had waited a millennium to be called to act. *He* had been waiting his entire life.

"Do not fear the future, Troy," the Herald who had visited his Station said to him when he'd brought word that they had been activated, *"Your destiny awaits."*

Troy wondered if the old man referred to the Wardens finally being called to act, or if the elder spoke of yet another legend. Troy had been shocked to say the least when the Herald had entered their tidy little Station in Virginia Beach with his flowing white hair. After he told them the news, he turned to Troy and recited another old tale.

"Young Thunderbird, you are the first to return us to Terra. Do not doubt your worth. Your destiny has been written in the stars since before you were born, Troy Waman. Remember, a Warden discovers his true measure when his fated mate is thrust upon him."

Whatever the fuck that meant. Troy looked down at his phone, then to the street sign on the corner, and finally, to the faded numbers painted on the mailbox in front of the ramble of a house his map app had brought him to.

Fuck, am I thinking? Fated mates are myths. Stories made up so orphaned Shifters would sleep through the night. He scoffed at the thought. Memories of tales the head nurse, Sr. Maria, had told him at the training camp he'd called home for years invaded his brain.

Memories were pesky things. Sometimes eternal, and always fucking portable. But he was no longer a child. *No more stories, Sister. Now, I act.*

"A thousand years we've waited, and I'm walking into a fucking scene from a bad episode of *Hoarders*," Troy shook his head and frowned at the decrepit house that sat a few hundred feet away from him.

It was cold as fuck outside and his leather jacket did little to warm him. Avian Shifters did not carry around the same bulk as other types of Shifters. He ran hotter than normals, but the single digit temperature froze him to the bone.

True, he wasn't beefy like some of his fellow Shifters, but he was just as incredibly strong, and he was wicked fast. Much stronger than any average male. He paused briefly gauging the atmosphere. There was something off about the place. He scented

Magic and something else. His Bird bristled beneath his skin. *Easy now.*

Lightning flashed in the darkened skies, allowing him to see the worn shingles, and cracked siding of the beaten-up colonial in greater detail. More than one window had been smashed and boarded up with cheap plywood.

If anything, it enhanced the creepy haunted house feel of the place. The porch sagged dangerously. He wondered how the place had managed to not be condemned by the town. One thing was certain, it was an ugly little turd of a house.

Who the hell put gray siding on their house anyway? Maybe it wasn't always that color. Maybe the owner liked gray. *Whatever.* He couldn't give two shits about the siding.

His only concern was the increased supernatural activity in the area over the past two weeks. Ever since the owner, a *Mrs. Renalda Curosi,* passed away. *A haunting?*

A creaking sound floated up to his ears and he stilled his movements. The sound developed into more of a *moaning* noise. An unearthly wail. It grew louder as the lightning continued to flash in the sky.

Troy had never seen a ghost. True, there were a

lot of things in the universe he had never seen nor heard of, but that didn't make them any less real.

If ghosts were real, and they made noises, he imagined that pitiful wail was damn close to what it would sound like.

No such thing as ghosts. Yeah, well, most people had never heard of Shifters either. And yet, there he stood.

His Thunderbird shifted once more beneath his skin, the beast flexing his senses as the lightning in the air drew him to the surface. *No.* He told his other half. His human needed to be in control now. He walked across the street, keeping to the shadows.

Something was indeed off about the creepy old house. He inched further to the black door. The knocker was in the shape of a face or mask. No discernible features, just a vague impression of eyes, nose, and mouth. *Shadowland indeed.*

He listened with his enhanced hearing and frowned. There was a distinct voice somewhere beneath the moaning and creaking. A *female* voice. His curiosity was piqued.

From what he'd seen in her file, Mrs. Curosi was ninety-seven when she passed. Her closest living relative was a half-sister, a *Magdelena Kristos*, and she lived over three hours away in New Jersey. The half-sister was cut from Mrs. Curosi's will recently. She'd bequeathed her entire estate, house, bank account, and all her earthly belongings, to someone named *A. Kristos. Another sister? Maybe.*

Troy hadn't given it much thought until now. A crash sounded from inside the house. He perked up as the feminine voice he'd thought he'd heard earlier screamed in pain. *Time to act.*

"Are you out of your mind?"

Xavier DuMont, Vampire and Prince of the Tenebris Clan out of DuMont, New Jersey, ran a hand
over his face. It was almost five in the morning on
Wednesday, and he was still going over the weekly
requests and complaints.

He could not believe it. One after the other, he'd
received dozens of requests for formal introductions
for most of the eligible young females in the Clan by
their parents or some family matchmaker or other. It
was the 21st Century, and yet, the Vampires of the
Tenebris Clan still thought he needed an arranged
marriage to run things!

"No, Lucius, I assure you my mind is sound."

"How can you be thinking of going away? To some retreat? At this time of year! You know, the whole Clan is up in arms over the tax laws your father had set into motion before his demise. Some are questioning your right to rule. Then, there is still the matter of your mating—"

"Lucius, for the love of fuck! I know what is going on in my own Clan. I am even now revoking those tax laws, people will just have to be patient."

"And what about meeting with these young females? Maybe that will quell some of the unrest—"

"No! I am not inclined to take a mate at this time. My father's grave has barely begun to grow grass. There is no rush!"

"There is pressure though, sire," Lucius Redwing insisted.

He was Xavier's oldest and most reliable friend. At nearly three hundred years old, they'd known each other for a considerable length of time. Lucius had been his childhood companion when they'd fled France for the New World. After settling the town of DuMont, his father had not only been the most productive of the local normals, but he had taken over their branch of the Clan.

Breaking ties with the old regime, and establishing their own rule, the DuMonts had done exceedingly well. Of course, coming into the new century had been difficult for some, but Xavier was determined to do it, to breathe new life into the old-fashioned world of Vampires. He would see them succeed and blossom in this age that was simply exploding with technology.

"I know you have plans, sire. But the anxious mamas are already parading their daughters resumes as if they were applying for a job." Lucius grinned. He waved a manila envelope bursting with applications for audiences with him from the most prestigious Vampire families in all of DuMont.

"For fuck's sake, Luc. Get rid of them," Xavier growled, and ran a hand over his face.

"Now, now. Surely, you know enough not to disrespect tradition and courtesy. These families are your staunchest supporters. Without their aid, your ascension to leadership could be challenged. The right mate would stop all of that—"

"I will not be forced into this, Luc. If anyone wants to challenge me for the right to lead, then he or she can face me out in the open. Not hide behind some political game."

"But sire—"

"No. I will not be manipulated. You should know that of me, old friend."

"Yes. Of course." Lucius nodded, placing the hefty envelope on the corner of Xavier's desk.

Vampires did not always inherit the right to lead. Princes were not born but made. Wasn't that what his father had always said? And yet, royal blood flowed in his veins. And it was because of that blood —*his royal DuMont blood*—that so many hungry mamas yearned to tie one of their young to him for eternity.

Fortunately, Xavier had avoided them. He refused to be pressured to take any of the hungry misses for his mate, as of yet. But with his recent ascension, that pressure was now on full keel.

Shit and fuck.

"I've got an idea," Lucius said, thrusting a copy of *The Nightly News* at him.

"What is it, Luc? I am in no mood."

"Read there," his friend said, pointing at an article on the bottom left.

"A retreat? I haven't been on one of those since I was ninety."

"Yes, but remember the fun? I brought my *sheep* at the time, and you pouted because I wouldn't share her!"

"As I recall, she came quite willingly to my bed when summoned, Luc. Why do they still call them sheep? My gods, that is positively medieval!" he replied.

"In case normals see the newspaper, of course."

"Impossible. The Covens bespelled the paper to only go to supes."

"It has happened, Xavier. You know this as well as I."

"True. And Luc, I am sorry about Temple. That was your donor at the time, was it not?"

"Temple? Yes. Not to worry, sire. You always did woo the ladies without trying. Besides, now they have their own donors on hand. You do not need to bring one."

"You don't have to do that, you know."

"What?"

"Calling me sire."

"I do have to call you sire, *sire*. You are my Prince."

"Oh, do shut up. I am your friend, Luc. You've known me my entire life."

"Yes, sire."

"Luc," he growled his friend's name.

"Shall I make the arrangements then?"

"Fine. I will go to this retreat for the weekend if

only to shut you up. And to get away from all this."
He indicated the pile of correspondence.

"Very good, sire."

"Are you fuckin' with me?"

"No, Randall, I assure you I am not fuckin' with you," Rafe Maccon eased his immense frame back into his oversized, black leather chair and narrowed his ice blue eyes at his Third and one of his oldest friends. How long had he known the man sitting in front of him?

Randall had come to Maccon City when Rafe was about ten, he looked the same then as he did now. Tall at six foot three inches, muscular, and more than a little intimidating to the Wolves under him with his long beard and equally long dark brown hair.

Rafe, however, was the Alpha. He was more amused than intimidated by his surly friend.

"A vacation?! What the fuck am I gonna do on a vacation? Come on, Rafe, this is bullshit!"

The door to Rafe's private office flew open and in strolled a very happy, very pregnant Charley Maccon, Rafe's wife. The Alpha's eyes glowed as they landed on his positively glowing mate. She wore a long, flowy dress. The shade was a pale-yellow color that, Randall admitted to himself, looked damn good with her creamy complexion and curly dark hair.

Their Alpha Female was quite something. There wasn't a Wolf Guard in the place who wouldn't lay down his/her life for her.

"Well, maybe you should consider a vacation to be a relaxing experience, Randy," she dropped a kiss on Randall's cheek and walked past him, over to her husband whom she kissed full on the mouth.

The way his Alpha's eyes homed in on her when she opened the door was nothing compared to the hungry gaze that followed her across the room.

Randall had noticed it took a while for Rafe to get used to his mate's habit of greeting everyone with a kiss or hug. Wolves were protective of their mates, but Randall thought his Alpha was doing an exceedingly good job of hiding his tension. Werewolves did not share very well.

Charley; however, had stood firm. That was the

way she was raised, and she wasn't going to change for any, how had she put it? Neanderthal brow-beating husband, regardless of how cute his ass was!

Randall had no direct knowledge if the "cute ass" statement was true or not. And he didn't want to know. He liked Charley though, had from the beginning. He was musically inclined and often took to one of the common rooms to strum his guitar or play a few keys on the piano.

ABOUT THE AUTHOR

C.D. Gorri is a USA Today Bestselling author of steamy paranormal romance and urban fantasy. She is the creator of the Grazi Kelly Universe.

Join her mailing list here: https://www.cdgorri.com/newsletter

An avid reader with a profound love for books and literature, when she is not writing or taking care of her family, she can usually be found with a book or tablet in hand. C.D. lives in her home state of New Jersey where many of her characters or stories are based. Her tales are fast paced yet detailed with satisfying conclusions.

If you enjoy powerful heroines and loyal heroes who face relatable problems in supernatural settings, journey into the Grazi Kelly Universe today. You will find sassy, curvy heroines and sexy, love-driven heroes who find their HEAs between the pages. Werewolves, Bears, Dragons, Tigers, Witches, Romani, Lynxes, Foxes, Thunderbirds, Vampires, and many more Shifters and supernatural creatures dwell within her worlds. The most important thing is every mate in this universe is fated, loyal, and true lovers always get their happily ever afters.

Want to know how it all began? Enter the Grazi Kelly Universe with Wolf Moon: A Grazi Kelly Novel or pick up Charley's Christmas Wolf and dive into the Macconwood Pack Novel Series today.

For a complete list of C.D. Gorri's books visit her website here:

https://www.cdgorri.com/complete-book-list/

Thank you and happy reading!

del mare alla stella,
    C.D. Gorri

Follow C.D. Gorri here:
    http://www.cdgorri.com
    https://www.facebook.com/Cdgorribooks

https://www.bookbub.com/authors/c-d-gorri
https://twitter.com/cgor22
https://instagram.com/cdgorri/
https://www.goodreads.com/cdgorri
https://www.tiktok.com/@cdgorriauthor